RIPPLER

Rippler

Book One in the Ripple Series

Cidney Swanson

For JWS

1

NEARLY DROWNED

The screaming was the first clue that I'd turned invisible again. Above the steady roar of the river, my teammates shouted: some with paddles flailing, others frozen mid-stroke. I'd never disappeared in front of anyone. Before this, I hadn't even known if it was real or if I was losing my grip on sanity. But now, surrounded by people who looked terrified, I knew it was real.

Which didn't exactly comfort me.

It wasn't until I heard Gwyn shouting about me *drowning* that I realized no one had actually *seen* me turn invisible. For a heartbeat, I felt relief—it wasn't real after all! But then I realized that the fact that people were staring straight at my position, aft, on the back of the raft, and *not seeing me* confirmed what I feared. My body had vanished.

And now I had an additional problem. If I came solid right now, someone would definitely see it happen. So did I want screaming because I'd drowned or screaming because I'd materialized out of thin air? Did I even know for sure *how* to get back inside my body?

"Calm down and look for anything orange," shouted Coach. "That'll be her helmet or her PFD."

"Her life vest will save her, right?" Gwyn asked.

"Not from entrapment," said Will. "We should get to shore. I'll hold the raft and you can send teams up and down the river to spot her in case she's trapped."

"Good thinking," said Coach. "Paddle for shore!"

My cross country team came to, redirecting the craft which had spun sideways. Coach set his own oar down and reached onto the sloshing floor for the rope tote-bag. Clipping the bag to his life vest, he began removing the coil.

The raft scraped against the graveled shore and everyone piled out.

If they all leave, I can reappear. I hope. It wasn't like this came with a manual.

"Whoever sees her first, use the whistle on your PFD," said Coach, pulling swim goggles from a pocket.

Hands flew to life-vests, fumbling for emergency whistles. Coach sent José and Nathan, the team's fastest runners, scrabbling upstream. Gwyn and Carly ran downriver. Unwinding the safety rope, Coach ran it around a sturdy-looking tree and handed the end off to Will.

"Use it as a belay under your arms," said Coach. "If you see me with her, down on your butt and dig your heels in."

Coach adjusted his goggles and then plunged his head under the icy flow.

As soon as Coach was submerged, Will called out in a loud whisper. "Sam! Samantha! Come back *now* while Coach has his head underwater." He stared straight at me, or rather through me. How did he know I wasn't drowning? Could he see me?

"C'mon, Sam!" he called. "You still there?"

He pulled a hand through his messy curls and squinted at the river. He couldn't see me.

Coach came up for air.

"Anything?" Will shouted to Coach.

Coach shook his head in response and plunged under once again.

Will swore. "Now, Sam! Unless you want the whole cross country team asking questions!"

That decided it: I preferred panic over drowned-Sam to panic over invisible-Sam. But did I know how to get back inside my skin again? I looked at Will's dark eyes, at the frown shrinking his mouth.

"Oh, God," said Will, his voice quieter this time. He looked scared.

Beside us, the Merced River roiled through the

canyon, indifferent to the fate of those who lived by breath. I had to let Will know I was safe. And then all at once, there I was, my body back solid, thighs stuck on the hard edge of the raft, feet planted on a bar above two inches of puddled water, an oar in my grip.

Will's face lit up. "Quick!" He reached for my hand, pulling me off the raft. "Take off your helmet."

"What?" I had questions for him, and none of them involved my helmet.

"I saw you—I know about what you can do," said Will, undoing the buckle on my orange helmet and hurling it upstream.

Coach's head re-emerged. The bobbing helmet caught his attention immediately and he swam out for it.

I opened my mouth to ask Will what he'd seen, what it was that he knew, but he began whistling madly, signaling everyone I'd been found.

I grabbed his arm, pulling him around to face me. "What just happened?"

He ignored my question, looking panicked as he ran his eyes over me from head to toe. "Oh, crap! You're dry."

He took my other hand, sprang to the river's edge, and shoved me so that I tumbled backwards into the shallows.

"What do you think you're doing?" I took water in through my mouth and nose, and then I couldn't stop coughing long enough to ask my questions.

"You need to look like you fell in," he said, splashing more icy water on me.

I hunkered down, still gagging, and held up the flat of my palm in a "stop" gesture.

Will quit as José and Nathan scampered down to us; they'd heard the whistle.

Will moved close, helping me up, and whispered loudly in my ear. "You rippled; you *vanished*. Say you fell in. Unless you'd rather be the six o'clock news."

I nodded, confused by the fact that Will was taking this so well.

Coach, swinging my helmet from one hand, emerged from the river, intense relief upon his browned face. "Sammy!" He used my childhood name as he wrapped strong, wet arms around me. "I was so worried! What would I have told your dad? Thank God you're okay." He released me and stepped back, looking me over. "You *are* okay, right?"

Glaring at Will, I said, "I'm fine, just a little wet—"

Will interrupted me. "She fell out and lost her helmet, but she's okay."

Coach handed the helmet to me as Carly and Gwyn joined us.

The next few minutes were a blur of my teammates hugging me, saying how good it was to see me alive, and arguing over what to do for a near-drowning victim.

The trip down the Merced River was Coach's idea

for team-bonding. Our men's and women's teams were too small to compete, and Coach had been looking for ways to keep our enthusiasm up and hopefully get us to recruit friends. I'd gotten Gwyn to sign up by telling her about the raft trip.

Now, seeing her turn back every couple of minutes to make sure I was still onboard, I figured she was questioning her decision. But as Coach shouted orders to us through a class four rapid, I heard Gwyn roaring above the river, "Yeah, baby, bring it on!" She swung back to me, black braids flying, during the post-rapid calm to give me a huge thumbs-up.

"Is this the best day ever, or what?" she shouted, grinning ear to ear.

I'd have to go with "or what," I thought. I gave her the best smile I had in me, but it must not have been very convincing.

"Oh, my God, Sam, I'm such an idiot!" said Gwyn.

Setting her oar down, she leaned back and threw an arm around my neck. "It's the worst day of my life. It totally sucks and I am completely hating every minute."

I hugged her back and told her to shut up.

Will, meanwhile, completely stonewalled me. Instead of turning back to speak with me, Will cracked jokes with Nathan and José. Coach announced we could take turns swimming for a couple of miles, and I was about to ask Will to jump out with me when he leaned across the raft and shoved Nathan in, then slipped out after him.

I wanted to hit Will over the head with the paddle. Inside my water-socks, my toes curled and uncurled. I needed answers about what *exactly* had happened earlier. What had Will seen? Or thought he'd seen? What was wrong with my body? And *why* did he think ignoring me right now was an option? I frowned at Will as Nathan tried to shove him under the water—impossible with the PFD.

A blistering sun, merciless, created pockets of contrast through the river. The bright-lit ripples and dark undersides of submerged boulders alternately caught my eyes. Above, the canyon narrowed, closing off the sky to a strip of intense blue. Walls of water-carved stone pressed in and the river began to churn once more, furious at confinement. I shuddered in the triple digit heat, feeling in this an echo of my own entrapment, pressed inside a body I didn't understand and couldn't control. This was the third time it had happened since school let out two months ago.

Coach called Will and Nathan back in. Will flashed me one tiny smile as he took his position in front of me once more. We lived a mile apart on the same highway just out of Las Abuelitas, and after meeting by accident a few times, we'd started running the two miles to school almost everyday as a warm-up before cross country practice.

But now, when I needed him desperately, I couldn't

get his attention. I thought about just saying out loud, in front of everyone, "Hey, Will, so what was that you said about people vanishing into thin air?" But I didn't. My own reputation among the kids I'd known all my life was finally on the upswing. I didn't need to start a whole new round of pointing and staring now that people were finally *not* talking about eight years ago.

Coach began shouting orders for the next set of rapids, a pair of boat-eating class fours. I jammed my feet farther under the bulging wall of the raft, feeling relieved to have something to do that took all my concentration.

When we reached the pull-out, Coach gave a speech about teamwork and how proud he was that we'd all worked together to prevent a tragedy. It took me a minute to realize I was the prevented-tragedy, and then I felt my face heating up. I mumbled thanks, feeling like a colossal liar. Will reached over and gave my shoulder a friendly squeeze. His smile was sober, appropriate to the solemn moment.

If I was a colossal liar, what did that make Will?

2

Q & A

As Coach explained his version of the day's events to Dad and Sylvia on the brick drive of our house, Will finally decided to acknowledge me.

"So I'll see you at six tonight for our run, okay?" he asked.

What run? I met his eyes, my own narrowing.

He raised one eyebrow and tipped his head slightly. The resulting look was somewhere between trying-too-hard and complete-idiot and made me laugh.

"See you at six," I agreed. "Here."

"Good to see you smile," he said and then pulled the van door shut.

I showered and put on clean clothes and tried to figure out how to tell Sylvia and Dad what had really happened. "Dad, Syl, guess who turned invisible today?"

That start didn't sound too promising. "So, you know how Coach told you I almost drowned? That didn't happen, but there's this other thing . . ." Not an improvement. Maybe I should tell them to sit down first. *Yeah, 'cause if you say that, they'll be thinking drugs or pregnancy, and vanishing into thin air will come as a relief.*

I wadded my still-damp rafting clothes into a tight ball and stuffed them deep in my laundry basket. Then I started picturing my laundry basket festering with hidden mold. Sighing, I dug out the tee and shorts and trudged down the stairs.

"Feeling refreshed?" asked Sylvia.

I nodded (an untruth) on my way to the washer. My step-mom was easier to talk to than my dad. Maybe I should start with her. But the words weren't coming.

"How's *Los Cabos* sound for dinner?" she asked.

My stomach was in knots. I didn't feel like Mexican. I didn't feel like ever eating again.

Sylvia's brow furrowed. "You sure you're okay?"

I shrugged. "I don't feel like going out tonight."

"There's leftover lasagna if you'd rather lay low," said Sylvia.

"Lasagna sounds perfect," I lied.

"I'll tell your Dad. We were just getting ready."

She hugged me tight and when she let go I took a deep breath.

"So, there's this thing I wanted to let you know," I said. Then my brain froze, like I'd stopped being able to speak in English.

Sylvia waited, smiling, eyebrows raised.

I completely chickened out.

"I, um, might go to bed early tonight." Another lie. I didn't see myself sleeping any time soon.

A few minutes later the house was empty except for me, assuming I was still solid. I looked into the hall mirror. *Still here.* I frowned at my messy bun, at the wet, dark strands escaping the elastic. My mom's grey eyes stared back at me; I looked away.

Just then I heard Will's knock—three quick taps. I ran to answer.

"We are *so* not running right now," I said, by way of greeting.

"Um, okay," said Will. "Are you home alone?"

"My folks are out getting Mexican for the next half hour or so."

"Maybe we should talk in your step-mom's garden."

"So you're finally in the mood to talk?"

"Geez, Sam," Will fidgeted with his cell, opening and shutting it. "I'm sorry. I just—listen, there's a lot to talk about, but most of it wouldn't sound so great in front of regular people."

"Regular people? Did you seriously just call me abnormal, *to my face*?" I punctuated the last words by poking Will's chest.

He smiled and brushed my hand aside. "You know

that's not what I meant."

"Come on," I said, sighing. I led him out the kitchen sliding glass door.

We crossed the deck, skirted the pool, and tromped down a set of railroad-tie stairs curving into a small ravine. A hint of a breeze wafted past in the warm evening air. At the raised beds flanked by a couple of scrawny apricot trees, I stopped and sat on a stone bench. Will grabbed a boulder opposite me.

"So spill," I said. "You said you knew about what I did? How? And why is this happening to me?" My heart beat out a crazy-fast staccato. I was about to get answers!

"Um, okay. So, number one—my sister studies what you do. Number two—you have abnormal genes."

"Again with the abnormal?" I asked.

His mouth formed a lop-sided smile. "You have genes for something my sister's advisor—well, former advisor—called *Rippler's Syndrome.* As in, you can ripple."

"Ripple?" I asked, puzzled by his repeated use of the unfamiliar word.

"Oh, sorry. You've never heard it called that. My sister actually invented the word to describe what you do: turning invisible. Or coming solid. The air shimmers a little—like a ripple on the water," he explained. "So your genetics make you able to ripple when you want to."

"When I *want* to?" I shook my head. "I wish!"

"You can't ripple when you want to?"

"It happens accidentally," I said. "And it's getting worse. I mean, I've noticed it two other times this summer."

"And never before that?" Will looked puzzled.

"I'm pretty sure it happened a couple of times right after Mom and Maggie's deaths. Not that I recognized it at the time. I can think of some times when I got in trouble for running off when I knew I didn't run off. So maybe I vanished then, too, and just didn't notice it."

He looked across at me, an anxious expression on his face. "You ever been diagnosed or seen a doctor about this?"

I laughed, making a kind of snorting noise. "Yeah, right, I just walked into Dr. Yang's office this afternoon and said I'd been having trouble misplacing myself."

"Really?" Will's eyebrows shot up in alarm.

"No, you dweeb," I said. "I can't even figure out how to start a conversation with Sylvia or Dad about this, much less Dr. Yang. He'd have me on heavy meds faster than you can say 'mental patient.'"

"So you haven't seen a doctor?"

"That's what I just said."

"That's really good news."

"Why? I thought you called this a medical condition."

Will dropped his eyes to a pair of lizards which zipped out in front of us, did a few push-ups and then zoomed away to safety.

"How do you know about this anyway?" I asked. "I've never heard of Rippler's Syndrome."

"No," said Will, scuffing his worn shoes in the dirt. "You wouldn't have heard of it. Only a handful of people have. And most of them are dead now."

"*You* are about to be dead for joking about this," I said, aiming one of my flip-flops at his head.

"I'm not joking, Sam. I wish I were."

"I'm going to die from this?" My stomach wrenched.

"No. I mean, not exactly. Give me a minute to explain. Okay, so, my sister Mickie was a biology major, right? After graduating, she worked for this genetics professor named Dr. Pfeffer. He studied a rare disease, Helmann's Disease, which acts sort of like leprosy, and Mickie wanted to study Helmann's because our dad had it. But secretly, the professor studied a special form of the disease resulting in what you have—the ability to ripple."

"Wait—what? I have leprosy?"

"No, no, forget I said leprosy. You have this other thing—the thing Mick's professor studied *in secret*. Dr. Pfeffer let her in on his research because of some, er, highly unusual circumstances. He'd been working alone for a decade. He swore Mick—well, both of us—to absolute secrecy because two of his previous colleagues were murdered. According to Pfeffer, they were killed because they were studying rippling, and someone out there doesn't want anyone to know about it, much less study it."

Above the garden, I heard the roar of my dad's truck. They must have decided on take out. Did I want to tell them everything right now or hear more from Will on my own? I hesitated.

Will continued. "Pfeffer believed that people with the rippling gene are in danger from this same person or group of people, so that's the risk I'm talking about. That's why you don't want to go spreading the word that you have this."

"Come with me," I said. My decision to hear Will out had just solidified. "So my folks don't interrupt us."

I dashed along a contracted path away from the garden and house. To the south, our land dropped away to a small canyon. Overlooking the canyon sat a patch of flat ground I claimed as "mine" when we moved here with Sylvia as my new step-mom five years ago.

Will and I flopped to the ground. The breeze felt weaker here, but the sun would be down soon. This was a place I came when I felt most alone, and I felt hollow inside as we settled. Maybe some of my old feelings had worked their way into the very soil, into the view, at least for me. I looked across the canyon, at the far foothills arranged in rows like a battalion, ending in the hazy distance of California's San Joaquin Valley. I tried to gather all the questions and fears into something I could talk over with Will.

He brushed a hand against my shoulder. "Sam? I know it's a lot to take in. Believe me, I get that, okay?" He looked at me, dark orbs piercing my fear and isolation.

I wasn't in this alone.

The question, when it tumbled out, surprised even me. "Why wouldn't you look at me on the raft?" I asked. "It was like you didn't want to acknowledge I existed."

Will kicked at the dirt. "You must have thought I was being a total jerk. I was so scared you'd start talking about rippling. I ignored you to try and keep you safe."

"To keep rumors from starting?"

Will nodded.

Trying to keep me safe was a million times better than ignoring me. A weight lifted off my chest.

"So can you put me in touch with this Pfeffer guy?" I asked.

"He's kind of . . ." Will looked down, fussed with a piece of his sneaker that was peeling away. "He's missing, presumed dead."

"Oh. I'm sorry for . . ." I heard the phrase tumbling out of my mouth, words that I swore I'd never say about someone dying, so inadequate. "Were you close?"

"He was our friend. And a good man."

In my head, I heard the worn out words like a recording: *Sorry for your loss; we're sorry for your loss; so sorry for your loss.* I turned the recording off. "So, maybe your sister could explain all this to my folks. They're gonna think I'm nuts when I tell them. Sylvia's doctor-happy as it is, and I'll need help convincing them both I don't need a psychiatrist."

Will jerked his head up swiftly, a look of worry creasing his forehead. "When you say 'doctor-happy,' that means what?"

I rolled my eyes. "An ingrown toenail is cause for a trip to Fresno's best podiatrist, that kind of thing."

"Then, you can't tell them. The risk of someone finding out is too great." His hands balled into fists so tight the skin began to whiten.

What he said was starting to make sense.

What was the first thing Dad or Sylvia would do assuming they didn't think I was crazy or lying? They'd take me to the doctor. And assuming I could vanish in front of a doctor, well, what would you do if you were a doctor, knowing you've hit the jackpot of medical history? Word would spread like a summer brush fire. If Will was right, I'd end up dead. Even if he was wrong, I'd end up a lab rat.

Either way, my life looked like a mess. I grasped at a last thread of hope. "Couldn't it be a coincidence that those researchers died?"

"Pfeffer was sure they were killed. And now he's gone, too. I wouldn't bet my life on it."

Goosebumps rose up and down my arm. Would I

bet my life on it?

"There's something else," said Will. "Pfeffer's disappearance has made my sister really paranoid. If we tell Mickie, she'd make it into this huge deal that you live here in town and that the killers might find you and then somehow discover where she and I are hiding out."

"You guys are in hiding? What, like the witness protection program?"

"Sort of, yeah. Minus the protection part. If you don't mind, I'd rather not tell Mick that you have the rippling gene. I think she'd make us move and . . . I like it here. A lot."

I didn't have a problem not telling his sister. She kind of intimidated me.

"I can pull some information together for you, scientific stuff, if you want," said Will.

"That would be helpful," I said.

Orange and gold now streaked the sky. Sylvia said it was air pollution that created the beautiful sunsets. Something beautiful from something bad.

I took a deep breath and snuck a glance at Will. He was fidgeting with a leaf and his eyes flickered briefly my direction.

He started tearing pieces off the leaf. "I hate to say it, but I should get back. My sister freaks when I bike or run on the highway after dark. Makes me want to shove my age in her face, but she knows I can't pay for my own place." He threw the rest of the leaf to the ground.

"Dude, you're what, sixteen? You can't move out on your own." I stood and we started back up to the house.

"Do I look sixteen?"

"Is this a trick question?"

Will looked at me, waiting for my answer.

"Yeah, you look sixteen."

"I'm eighteen actually. We . . . moved around a lot, and I got behind in school. Plus I kind of missed a year when Mom got sick. So I'm an eighteen-year old sophomore."

"And you're still in school? Are you insane?"

He shrugged. "I want a good education. It mattered to Mom. Anyway, I can't leave Mick. She's all I've got," he said.

"Not all," I said, punching his shoulder.

He looked over, a half smile on his face. "Not all."

As soon as Will left, the questions began multiplying. Things I couldn't believe I hadn't thought to ask: stacks of Sam-questions piling up in my head like boxes in a warehouse. The big ones were pretty basic: Could I prevent this from happening? Could I get "stuck" invisible forever? Was Rippler's Syndrome dangerous, apart from possible murderous intentions of mysterious bad guys?

Will and his sister shared a small cabin and one cell

phone. If I texted questions, she might be the one who read them. She'd hear every word if I called. And Will had dropped enough hints about her hyper-vigilance that I didn't want her asking him why he had to go outside to talk on the phone.

In the end I composed a carefully obscure text which could be seen as me asking about homework— we had a summer research assignment for AP Biology this coming fall.

He didn't respond until after midnight, but I was still wide awake.

Experience helps. I have some ideas.

Getting stuck not an issue.

Not dangerous.

Even with these three most important questions answered, I didn't sleep, and that took me back to the sleepless months after the hit and run. Some nights I'd lain awake wishing I could die; other nights I'd been terrified I'd be killed, too.

And now, according to Will's vanished professor-friend, I had a real reason to be afraid. I would have to spend the rest of my life hiding this ability.

Experience helps.

I didn't have much. I hoped the papers Will was gathering for me included an instruction manual. But *I have some ideas* sounded like he was just going to offer advice based on his sister and Pfeffer's research. Obviously I'd take whatever I could get, idea-wise. The possibility that I might ripple at school sent another flood of adrenaline through me. I sat upright. My clock read 2:23 AM.

I wondered if Will was sleeping. It must have been a shock to see a living, breathing example of a rippler. The more I thought about it, the weirder the coincidence sounded. Las Abuelitas was a very small town. He must have been surprised.

2:42 AM.

Was Will worried for me? Losing sleep over it?

I burrowed back under my duvet, curled on my side, and drew my legs up into my chest. I'd slept this way after I lost Maggie and Mom. It felt safe.

3:04 AM.

I thought about the panicked look on Will's face beside the river, before I'd come back solid, and his whispered words of fear. *He really cares about me.* I smiled and uncoiled my body. I'd wondered before if Will felt something special for me. Sometimes I'd caught a glance that felt different from "just friends."

3:29 AM.

But everyone else from my team had looked really concerned at the river, too. It was a natural response.

4:09 AM.

What am I doing wondering if Will likes me? Do I not have enough on my plate at the moment?

At 4:32 AM, I staggered outside to sit on the deck. The pool waterfall was turned off and all was quiet.

Overhead, the stars glistened and shimmered, impossibly numerous against a raven-black sky. Panic slowly receded.

But by breakfast, I didn't look so good, and Sylvia noticed.

"You want to cut today? I can call Coach," she offered. "We want you ready for school next week."

"No." I was desperate to see Will. "I want to run."

Will knocked at the door, and we were off.

"Wow, you look awful," Will said as we headed up the driveway.

I didn't respond.

"Hmm. Awkward," said Will.

"No, it's okay. I'm sure I look like a zombie. I had trouble sleeping."

"So, your folks, did you talk to them?" he asked.

"No. If I had, I'd be in some medical office right now, getting my blood drawn or my brain scanned or something."

Will nodded. "I'm glad you're not telling; my sister's too paranoid about some things, but I don't think this is one of them."

"Did you tell her about me?"

"I thought about it. I stayed up 'til past two trying to decide."

"And?"

"I'm not going to. I'm sure she'd make us move. It's just how she is, ever since . . ." He left the thought unfinished, but I knew what he meant. Sometimes you just didn't want to speak your losses aloud.

Scaring up pairs of redwing blackbirds, we thumped along our quiet highway, running in perfect step with one another. The rhythm comforted me.

"Thanks for responding last night," I said. "To my questions."

"Oh, yeah. Sorry it took so long. I was pulling stuff together for you, and trying to keep off Mick's radar, and I didn't notice your text 'til late."

"I was just relieved to hear I'm not going to die from this . . . thing."

Will grinned. "That's good news, huh?"

"So what do you know about controlling what I do? School's starting and all."

Will nodded, taking a swallow from his Camelbak. "I've been trying to figure out how it is you rippled without meaning to. That's a little strange, from what I've read."

"Strange can't be good," I said.

"Well, I don't know. You said you've only disappeared a handful of times?"

"Yeah. Three times this summer. Before that, there's one other time I'm sure of when I was seven."

"What happened? Where were you?" asked Will.

"I was at a zoo with my grandma so I wouldn't ask questions about the cremation. I remember watching polar bears swimming. You could see them in this peaceful room below ground where my grandma had wheeled me in a stroller.

"I didn't know whether I was watching something real or a movie, but it didn't matter. That mass of white fur, those dark eyes flying toward the glass, toward me, and then spiraling backwards and away—I don't remember any other sounds or people. Nothing but those silent bears sailing towards me and away from me. I remember feeling warm and calm for the first time since the accident.

"I didn't notice the voices right off. But when the bears left the pool, suddenly it was noisy and people were calling my name. I twisted in my stroller to try to find my grandma and this woman looked at me like she was shocked to see me in the stroller. She asked if I was Samantha and she ran and got my grandma, who'd been far up the stairs away from me. And Grandma was really upset and crying and she told me to never run off like that again which didn't make sense to me, but I kept my mouth shut because she looked so unhappy. I didn't explain that I hadn't left the stroller. I didn't ask her why she had left me alone in the polar bear room. And I didn't understand the event. 'Til now."

Will took another sip and gestured that I should do the same.

It felt hot already and the water soothed my dry throat.

"Sam, I want to ask you something kind of

personal," Will said. "You don't have to answer."

I nodded, rubbing sweat from my forehead.

"After your mom and your friend were killed in that accident, were you depressed for a long time, maybe until just recently?"

I flushed. The question hit close to home. I didn't answer right away, just breathed in the scent of bear clover, strong already in the August heat, like artichoke and fresh-cut wood. When I spoke, my voice was husky with emotion.

"I pulled inside myself for a long time. You wouldn't know this because you didn't grow up around here, but I stopped talking to anyone for a couple of years. I got called shy or stuck-up, and those were the nice things kids had to say about me." I paused. The next part was harder to admit. "Gwyn Li was my friend, but then she moved to L.A. and lived there 'til just last year, when she and her mom moved back and opened the bakery. She didn't know about my . . . my weird years, so we just picked back up being friends. Then you came along this summer and now I have two friends."

"Geez, Sam. That's a long time to be alone."

I nodded and we ran in silence for a minute before I felt ready to say more.

"These last few months, I've finally felt happy again," I said. "I'd forgotten what it felt like, waking up and being excited about getting on with my day. I mean, running has always helped with the depression, but only when I'm running, you know?"

"Sure," said Will. "I think I understand why you started rippling this summer."

"Because I'm happy?"

"More or less," Will replied. "Wow, we're making good time."

I hadn't been paying attention, but Will was right. Murietta Park was coming up on our right: we'd reached Main Street already. We rounded past a hundred year old stand of willows. I held my hand out and ran it through the leafy branches.

"You do that every day," said Will.

I smiled. "Every time. Ever since I was—I don't know, actually. I've always done it. The leaves feel like dry water when you do it at a run."

"*Dry* water?" He raised an eyebrow.

I smiled and nodded. "If you could imagine water running over your hands and it was dry, that's what it would feel like."

Will shook his head, grinning.

I was bummed we'd have to stop talking in the next few minutes. I wanted to cram in more questions. "So yesterday you said I had a special form of genetic disorder?"

"Oh, right. So, usually, someone with this abnormality in their genes develops Helmann's Disease, which causes sporadic full-body numbness."

The hairs on my arms prickled as I remembered

something. "Will, I had a great-grandma who used to go all numb—to where she couldn't feel anything. They called it a type of leprosy. But she would go months without any symptoms, and she never did any damage to herself like lepers do."

Will nodded. "People with this chromosome often get told they have leprosy. Or it gets mixed up with psychosomatic numbness. But the symptoms of Helmann's Disease are pretty distinct once you get seen by a doctor. With Helmann's, you have to be totally chilled, happy basically, and then *whole body* numbness sets in. The 'happy' factor is one of main things a doctor looks for to make sure it's Helmann's Disease. That's what the genes do *normally*, okay? Your body has taken the disease and done it one better: you don't just go numb, you lose your physical being."

"When I get too . . . happy?" I asked.

"When your serotonin levels spike."

The track loomed ahead. I could see a few team members filling water bottles.

"So how come I don't vanish when we're running together?"

I felt my face turning red because of all that could be inferred from my question, but Will just answered it straight-faced. "You're using too much of your body's available energy when you run. It takes energy to ripple, and there's not enough left, I'd guess."

I nodded as we pulled into the school parking lot.

"So if I start to feel too happy, just take off running?"

Will guffawed. "You could try that."

We'd reached the track, which meant no further discussion for now, but we asked Coach to run us together. Coach liked to mix up men and women by pairs for Monday's timed runs, claiming it made the boys run harder (so a girl didn't beat them,) and it made the girls realize what they were capable of.

Half an hour later, after warm-up laps and a talk about staying hydrated, Coach released us onto the 7K, my favorite trail, even in the August heat.

I began rattling off questions as soon as we got out of earshot. It was harder to talk on a timed run, but I needed answers more than I needed a personal best. "Do I have Helmann's Disease, too?"

"You can't have both," panted Will. "Mick says one or the other shows up, but not both."

"And it's rare?"

"Helmann's is rare, rippling is ultra-rare."

"And my version is called Rippler's Syndrome."

Will nodded. We had to stop talking as we climbed through a shady mix of blue oak and digger pines. The digger pines weren't impressive like the nearby giant sequoias tourists flocked to see each summer, but I loved their ghostly-gray needles and charcoaled-bark. Mom had called them survivors; they defied the blistering summers that withered our foothill grasses and California golden poppies.

We reached the long flat stretch that ran across the side of the hill and Will spoke again. "Of course, officially, no one is studying Rippler's Syndrome at the moment. It's just a name Mick and Pfeffer used. You won't find anything if you look online."

"So who named it? Are they dead?"

Will looked embarrassed. "I named it."

"Oh. Cool."

We curved around a small bend and Las Abuelitas winked at us through a stand of dead pines burned out ten years ago. The skeletal shapes left behind were creepy, even in daylight. The trail narrowed after the burnt stretch to where only one person could run. I let Will go in front.

We now had a flat mile-and-a-half where talking would be easier.

"How common is this gene?" I asked.

"Mick could give you a scientific answer. All I know is it's rare."

Will was panting pretty hard from the last uphill stretch; my questions were short. Some of his answers were long.

"It's really, really rare," he continued. "But obviously not so off-the-charts rare that no one ever studies it. I mean, they invented a drug right after World War II that subdues the *numb-ness* form—Helmann's." He frowned and took a long pull of water. "I think I mentioned my dad has the disorder."

I nodded.

"His drug habit started because he didn't want to take his Neuroprine prescription."

"Does he ripple?"

"No. Thank God. He only experiences numbness—regular Helmann's."

"What a name, huh? Hell-man's?"

"Named after a scientist. He deserved the name," Will said, breathing hard. "He ran a science lab in Nazi Germany, and he wasn't known for his humane treatment of the patients he studied. After the war ended, he was accused of experimenting on children, but he either killed himself or escaped, so he wasn't tried."

"And what about a prescription? For me, I mean? Would it help?"

Will shook his head. "I honestly don't know if it would help with Ripplers or not. But, Sam, getting a prescription for that drug—it's like putting a big bull's-eye on your forehead. 'Hello, here I am, I've got the gene for Helmann's and possibly Ripplers.' Mick's professor theorized that the person or group killing Rippler's carriers uses prescription records to locate their targets."

"Got it," I said, a shiver running along the back of my neck. "No meds."

"There's other reasons to avoid Neuroprine," said Will. "It causes some pretty undesirable side-effects."

"Don't worry. You had me at, 'they'll find you and kill you.'" I chewed my lower lip. A prescription that took away the vanishing *would* have been awfully nice. "How sure are you I can learn to control this?"

"I'm sure," said Will. "I pulled some materials together for you. A lot of it is pretty dry reading, but there's evidence that people who ripple learn to control it. You just haven't had much experience yet."

I nodded. "Due to my extended residency in the Pit of Despair."

Will looked at me funny. "You don't have to make a joke out of it. There's nothing embarrassing about depression."

I felt tears stinging my eyes. I blinked them back. "Thanks," was all I said.

"We'd better pick it up on the stretch downhill," said Will. "I can hear Carly and Nathan catching up to us."

"Okay," I said, pushing myself.

"Want to go to the Las ABC after? To look stuff over?" asked Will.

The Las Abuelitas Bakery Café had booths with high sides and lots of privacy. And every good thing made of butter and sugar.

"I'd love to," I said. It was practically a date. We approached another narrow stretch and I shouldered my way in front, thundering across a single-file wooden bridge.

"No fair!" said Will.

I laughed, my legs pumping crazy-fast.

Coach was shaking his head and glaring as we pulled past him, completing the 7K. "Not good enough, Ms. Ruiz, Mr. Baker."

Coach gave the two of us trash detail after practice for twenty minutes, which meant all the warm water was gone by the time I got to the lockers. That was okay; I was hot. I was thirsty, which meant I was already dehydrated. I felt exhausted, but my heart sang. Will had my back and things were going to be fine.

3

LITTLE BLACK BOOK

I looked through rippled glass set into the river-rock wall of Las ABC, the place Gwyn's mom opened last year. Will grabbed the front door, which held a massive oval of beveled glass set in an oak frame, hand-carved and probably paid for in gold-dust from Bella Fria Creek back during the California Gold Rush. We slipped inside.

It smelled intoxicating—like Sylvia's kitchen at Christmas: brown sugar, butter, and cinnamon. On the bakery-case bottom row sat thick-frosted brownies, layer cakes, and a berry pie—probably *syllaberry*, the drought-tolerant hybrid my dad invented. The middle row displayed cookies, all at a kid's eye level. Monster cookies with M&Ms. Snickerdoodles. Crinkled molasses cookies. And at my eye-level? Doily-ed plates of pastries: European bear claws and croissants beside Mexican *pan de huevos* and cinnamon-sugar coated *polvorones*.

I'd spent most of my allowance here the past year.

Gwyn waved, helping guests with her mom, Bridget, who remembered me from before and still called me Sammy. As Will and I waited to order, a fluffball cat wrapped himself around my legs, purring.

Will leaned in, saying, "I'll go grab that last booth."

"Don't you want anything?" I asked.

"Ice water?" He dropped down to retie a broken shoelace to itself. "I'm not really hungry." He gave me a smile, stood, and walked back to the booth.

I frowned; I knew Will and Mick didn't have much. My own allowance was ridiculous, way more than I needed. Would he feel insulted if I bought him something?

I ordered an ice water, a syllaberry bubble tea, and two orders of *polvorones*. Bridget grinned and popped two quarters into a large jar labeled "Feline Assistance Fund" on the counter.

The grey fluff-ball at my feet meowed, and Bridget noticed him as she handed me a flyer. "You naughty cat. Why can't you stay in the kennels?"

I smiled, taking the flyer. It announced an event called "Panning for Felines" happening on Labor Day.

"Rufus is not allowed in the bakery, Gwyneth," said Bridget. "How many times do I have to tell you?"

"Like I'm the boss of him," Gwyn replied.

"Grab the register while I make a bubble tea," Bridget said to Gwyn, dashing to the kitchen. "And get Rufus out."

"I did *not* let him in, Ma," Gwyn said. "Did she hit you up for the gold panning fundraiser yet?"

I waved the flyer in reply.

"You have a new best friend." She pointed to Rufus, purring loudly at my feet. "He's adoptable, you know."

"I'm not what you'd call a 'cat-person,'" I reminded her.

"Cats aren't for everyone. Only, don't say that in front of Ma," she said, rolling her eyes. "We're up to fifteen or sixteen in the cattery. I forget. Hence, the fund raiser." She pointed to the stack of colored flyers. "We need pledge sponsors for each hour we pan in case we don't find much gold."

"You'll find flakes," I said. "Maybe nuggets."

Gwyn's eyebrows shot up.

"I mean, not *huge* nuggets."

"No, no, no—not that!" Gwyn's voice dropped to a loud whisper and she tipped her head towards Will. "Are you guys finally dating?"

"Just . . . homework," I said.

"Oh, and me working all day," she said, shaking her head in mock regret.

I smiled. Gwyn acted like she hated school, but she

pulled straight A's.

She reverted to the whisper. "Homework—ha! I'm so asking Ma to tell me everything about Will. Ma's always chatting with the big sister."

"You mean Mickie?"

"Mmm-hmm," said Gwyn, eyes drifting back to Will. "It's still a date, even if you're doing homework."

"Shut up!" I said, lowering my own voice.

A guest walked up and handed Gwyn a twenty and a ticket.

"Keep the change," said the customer.

"God forbid I keep any for a tip," Gwyn murmured, popping the change into the cat jar. She moved on to help a customer who'd just arrived just as Bridget brought out my drink.

"Gwyn!" Bridget said. "Rufus?"

"I got him," I said. Cautiously, I picked up a cat for the first time in eight years and carried him to the front door, setting him outside quickly.

"We'll talk soon," said Gwyn, winking as I grabbed my cookies and drinks.

I rolled my eyes and walked over to Will. He was bent over a small black book and had placed two manila folders on my side of the table.

"What's that?" I asked, passing his ice-water across the table. "Your diary?"

"It's my sister's. It was Pfeffer's."

"You're reading her diary? Or Pfeffer's diary?"

"It's not a diary. At least I don't think it is. It was in that folder," he said, tapping the one to my right. "Those are all things Pfeffer gave us for safekeeping before he disappeared."

"So this will tell me everything I ever wanted to know about . . . myself?" I looked at the two folders.

"Yeah, I just grabbed everything in the end. I didn't want Mick catching me looking through her stuff."

"I'll be really careful with it," I promised. I wasn't the most scientifically curious of students, but I vowed to read every scrap of paper in those folders. "And I'll get it back by Wednesday, okay?"

"Uh-huh," he said.

He was really distracted.

"So what is it?" I pointed to the black book and grabbed a bit of *polvorone*.

"Some book of riddles. I don't think it's actually related to what Mick or Pfeffer studied. Maybe it's math problems." He scratched his head, eyebrows drawn tight in concentration as he looked down at the tiny handwriting.

"Let's hear one of them."

He looked at me, raised an eyebrow, and flipped back a couple of pages. "Here's the first one:

Twelve children and every morning, twelve knots of brown bread and twelve cups of warm cow's milk. Then one morning, eleven brown rolls with eleven cups of milk. There are still twelve children. What will happen?

"But that's dumb," said Will as he raked fingers through his dark hair. There's no divisors you can use with eleven. It's a prime number."

"How about this?" I offered. "Ten of the kids can eat whatever, but one is gluten-intolerant, so you give her the milk, and one is lactose-intolerant so you give her the bread. Everyone's happy."

Will laughed. "That's better than what I was thinking. I pictured a fight."

"Math books aren't so big on fights."

Will flipped to the next page. "Listen to this one. *'Ten children rest under ten blankets of eider-down. One chill morning the eider-downs are taken to be cleaned. Five filthy lengths of scratchy wool are brought in while the children march outside in snow. What will happen this bitter night?'"*

"Whoever wrote this has serious issues! What's with all the filth and scratching?"

Will cracked up. His laugh was deep and throaty. "Okay," he said. "One more:

'A bowl of poisoned water sits on a table before eight thirsty children. As their thirst increases, they try the door, but it remains locked.

What will happen when thirst drives them mad?'"

"That's twisted. Your sister's advisor had a psycho math book."

"I'd say it's no math book," replied Will. "See this?" He pointed to a section in blue ink. "That's Pfeffer's handwriting. He was translating this. Or he was trying to. He didn't get very far."

"Is the whole book like that?" I asked.

"Only the first couple pages have English translations scribbled down." Will flipped through a few more pages. "It's sort of like French, maybe. See here? 'Les enfans'—"

"The children," I said. "But it's spelled wrong."

"Right," agreed Will.

He puzzled over a couple more pages while I drank my bubble tea. I smiled, remembering the first time I'd noticed him in French class last year when our pregnant teacher's water exploded all over the ugly brown-and-grey linoleum. Everyone but Will wanted to puke; Will helped her to the office.

"I think I'll hold on to this book," said Will. "But you read through everything else, and let me know if you have questions."

I pushed the plate with the remaining cinnamon polvorones towards Will. "I'm done. This bubble tea is really filling."

Will stuffed one in his mouth and grunted a thank you, still poring through the black book. "This is some weird stuff," he said, stopping on another page with a long section in blue-inked English.

Gwyn walked past, winking at us. Will didn't see it, fortunately.

Will's cell vibed loudly from inside his pack. He flipped it open and frowned. "It's my sister. She sent me a text from *online*. That's creative." He scrolled through the message. "She wants to know where her stuff is. *This* stuff," said Will, tapping the packets in front of me. "Unbelievable. She hasn't looked at any of this for months and now she needs it?" He shook his head.

I pushed the manila folders back, one at a time. It felt like they weighed two hundred pounds each. I wanted that information so badly it hurt.

"Hey," said Will. "I think Mick's helping at some all-day plant sale this Saturday. I could get everything back for you and we could go somewhere. You want to go to Yosemite?"

I smiled. "I haven't been in forever."

Will stuffed everything back in his pack, and I texted Sylvia to come get us. She showed up a few minutes later in her TT, greeted Will, and tossed me the keys.

"Really?" I groaned.

"A woman needs to know how to drive a car with a clutch." It was something she said all the time. That, and, *a woman needs to know how to use a can of pepper spray.*

"A woman should not have to embarrass herself in front of her teammates," I said to Will as we stuffed ourselves in the tiny Audi. "Get ready for a bumpy ride."

Will and Sylvia did all the talking as I drove to his house. I had to concentrate to keep from killing the engine at the stop signs. I sent clouds of exhaust into the air each time, revving the car to keep it from dying. And as I watched the toxic clouds dissipating in the rearview mirror, I found myself wondering what kind of person would jot down sick riddles about bowls of poisoned water and thirsty children.

Excerpted from the private journal of Girard L'Inferne, circa 1939

Experiment 23, Control Group A

Twelve hands grab at the basket of rolls and one comes up empty. The tray of tin cups is set down. Twelve hands reach and two close on opposite sides of the last cup.

"What does it mean?" the children ask one another.

The two who hold the cup battle. Fritz wrenches the cup free after kicking the other child. But the milk splatters everywhere.

"What does it mean?" the children ask again, faces turned to Franz, the clever one, who is also the best in a fight.

"It means that if it happens again tomorrow, the last two can fight for it. The winner eats."

Weeks pass and some of the children begin to hope for days when not enough food is served. Others realize they can force a fight by taking an extra roll.

How swiftly and how well the children learn the lessons they are set.

-translation by G. Pfeffer

4

ILLILOUETTE CREEK

Dad wasn't real big on me going anywhere with Will, and I got an earful of that through the ducting that goes from our kitchen to my bedroom. He and Sylvia were arguing; I was making my bed—not an everyday occurrence—while waiting to hear the outcome. Will would come by in an hour.

"I'm not saying his dad isn't a drug-addict," said Sylvia. "But his sister is the one with custody, and she's doing a great job raising Will. She brought him here to *protect* him from their dad."

That was the rumor, but I knew *now* what else Mick was protecting Will from. I heard Sylvia rapidly tapping her foot. She does this when she's really irritated but doesn't want to come right out and say you're an idiot.

I couldn't make out my dad's response, but Sylvia's

43

foot tempo increased.

"Sam's going to Yosemite," she said. "Will's a great kid. He's a good friend to Samantha, and we both know Sam needs friends."

My dad sighed long and loud; I had no trouble hearing that. Then he conceded. "Long as he gets her back before nine."

My curfew was eleven, but I guessed Dad needed to win at something. I smiled. He was a good man. More in love with crops than people at times, but that's what made him a successful farmer.

My cell buzzed with a text. Will's sister was coming with us. I frowned and slapped at my comforter, trying to make it lie flat. This changed everything. I kicked a lone flip-flop across the floor. It stopped short of my open closet. Scowling, I walked over, picked up the sandal, and threw it into the back of the closet, slamming the door shut.

Mickie was fine in the abstract. She'd even been by the house a few times to trade plant starts and gardening tips with Sylvia. But why couldn't she have stuck to her plan of hanging out at the plant sale all day?

I sighed. *It is what it is.*

Sylvia somehow squashed two six-packs of Gatorade, two bags of chips, and a small cheesecake on ice into my day pack. Will was bringing sandwiches. Dad asked me three separate times about my cell: did I have it with me, was it charged, was the ringer on? It was annoying, but I gave him a big hug and told him I'd be fine. Then I saw him frowning at Will and wished I could take the hug back.

"Samantha, do you get car-sick?" Mickie asked as we finished loading the Jeep.

"Sometimes, a little," I admitted.

"Okay," she said, "Will drives and you ride up front. Narrow, curvy roads don't sit well with Will. He hurls if he's not driving."

"Mick—geez," Will groaned.

I chortled, then turned it into a throat clearing as I climbed in beside Will. I'd found Mickie's abrupt manner intimidating in the past, but she was kind of funny.

We began the drive, crawling through Oakhurst, Sugar Pine and Fish Camp.

"The Valley's going to be full," said Will, pointing at the line of hulking RV's ahead of us. "How about we stay up top? The high country will be less crowded and a few degrees cooler."

"Illilouette?" asked Mickie.

Will nodded. "Illilouette is this great waterfall that people never see because you have to hike in to find it. Above the falls, there's a beautiful stretch of creek. Mostly hikers think of it as something to get across, not an actual destination. Which is fine by us, eh, Mick?"

Mickie nodded, grinning.

The Jeep gained elevation and the digger pines disappeared; sugar and ponderosa pines took over. Shrubs and greener ground cover replaced yellow, dry grasses. When we reached Wawona at four-thousand feet, the air was fresher, cooler, scented by resinous pine with the hint of horses and barns nearby. I felt excited. "Wawona" and "Illilouette" were names I knew from my mom's paintings of Yosemite.

An hour later we pulled into the large parking lot at Glacier Point and scampered up to the trailhead. I gawked at the overlook, recognizing Half Dome at once; even in profile it was unmistakable. To the right of it, I could see two thin, bright ribbons of white that had to be waterfalls.

"Nevada Fall up top, Vernal Fall below," Will said when I asked if either of those were the waterfall we'd be hiking to. "Illilouette, our fall, is hidden below us."

Knobbly domes of granite perched everywhere, the spaces between filled by the dark greens of pines and brush. Far in the distance I could see jagged peaks, covered with snow even in late August.

Mickie asked politely if I wanted to walk out to Glacier Point itself. I didn't. I said I had a memory of standing there with Mom, and she dropped it. "We should probably get going anyway," Mickie said. "We want time to hang out plus the time it takes to hike there and back again."

The climb down to the creek was lovely. The path

had been well-maintained. "Our donations at work," said Mickie. She explained that the National Park itself couldn't afford the upkeep on all the hundreds of miles of trails and that an organization collected donations to help out.

We saw a few other hikers, mostly smiling backpackers coming out from the high country with a week's worth of grime and sunshine on their faces. The trail was far from quiet, however.

"Hear the waterfalls?" called Will, ahead of me on the path.

"It sounds like the ocean—like waves crashing," I replied. We rounded another switchback and the reverberation changed, becoming like a thousand voices whispering together. Nearer, I noticed smaller noises: the crunch of ground granite beneath my feet and the slap of webbing straps as my pack jostled.

The trail descended rapidly, carving through brush and thickets. We could see the burned out remains of pines, but shade was infrequent.

"I didn't think it would be so hot, just hiking downhill," I said as we stopped at an icy rivulet crossing the trail.

Mickie smiled and handed me a scrunchy. I put my hair up, and the breeze on my damp neck felt like heaven.

As we descended into the valley of the Illilouette Creek, the ponderosas clustered into a forest which provided shelter from the intense sun. The wind rumbled through the branches above us, and I felt small and insignificant beneath the murmuring giants. The trail continued in relentless zigzags to the creek below, changing from granite-gravel to dark, rich soil.

And then the trail diverged, without the rusted metal trail markers we'd seen at other forks. I paused, confused. Will passed me taking the left path, and Mick passed me to the right.

"My side has the view," Will called back to me.

"My way's faster," Mick hollered.

I followed Will. The brush cleared and I inhaled sharply at the vista. Before us, Illilouette Creek twisted ninety degrees and plunged to become a waterfall. We stood without speaking, watching the churning water as it raced to the cliff's edge and over falling down, down, down. If I fixed my eye on a bit of spray, it appeared to tumble in slow motion, like it wanted to avoid the inevitable crash. It made my throat clench and I felt sad somehow.

"Three-hundred-seventy foot drop," Will said. He looked over, caught my expression before I could hide it. "Hey, let's go find a place to sit and eat." He punched my shoulder and I smiled. We continued down the path, our shoes kicking up moist, earthy smells.

Through the trees, I caught flashes that had to be water. Soon Will and I were bouldering, scrabbling alongside the creek looking for his sister.

"Found her," Will called to me.

A patch of gravelly sand had collected on the side of the creek where Mickie waited, hands on hips, her back to us. We tumbled the packs off our shoulders.

"The water's so loud," I said. "I can't believe they call this a creek."

"Loud but peaceful," Will said.

Mickie turned to us, smiling. The spot she'd picked had a great view up the creek, where the water coursed white and foaming through boulders. The view downstream was blocked by a "snag," the term Mickie used to describe the fallen tree trunks piled atop one another along the creek. The snag backed the water up, creating a pool maybe six feet deep.

The creek-bottom was filled with varying sizes of rounded granite river-rock, uniformly speckled with black. Instead of ordinary whitish granite, I could make out a dozen different shades: ivory, gold, pinky-yellows, pale oranges, tans. The multi-colored rock tinged the water so that it appeared rosy-golden as it rushed downstream.

Mom would have known how to paint those colors.

Mickie had been quietly emptying her pack and now passed a sandwich to me. From my pack, I grabbed potato chips and drinks to share.

Half an hour later, sated and tired, the three of us collapsed: me onto gravel, Mickie against a boulder, and Will against a fallen trunk. I lay on my belly, warm and drowsy from food and the rushing noise of the creek.

After a few minutes sitting in silence, Mickie stood. "I need to take care of something 'one-hundred yards or more away from a fresh-water source.'"

I smiled. Mick had a way with words. The day was turning out better than I'd expected. I felt so relaxed I didn't even jump into twenty-question-mode once she was out of earshot.

Beside me, Will searched through a group of smaller rocks and pebbles. "Sorry about the change in plans," he said.

"It's okay. I'm having a great day. I like your sister's sense of humor."

"Sense of humor? She doesn't have one. But she's plenty funny."

I laughed at his assessment. "What are you looking for?"

"Skipping stones," he replied. He continued moving the rocks back and forth, removing one every so often and setting it aside in a growing pile.

"Look at this," he said, passing me a spherical piece of granite the size of a ping-pong ball.

"It's perfect," I said. The black speckles caught the sunlight and glistened as I turned it over.

"Keep it," said Will.

"You want to think twice giving a girl a big sparkly rock."

Will grunted, a small laugh.

I leaned out towards the creek and dipped the tiny globe to see what it would look like. Wet, the black spots leapt out in sharp contrast to the creamy background. I turned it to reveal splotches of pale gold. I set it in front of me in the pea-gravel to dry and gazed contentedly at the colorful rocks beneath the slick-smooth surface of the water. Sunlight splattered through tree limbs high overhead, dotting the creek with bright splotches as it flowed inexorably to the falls. I'd never seen anything so lovely, so hypnotic.

Will set another round rock beside my first one. I smiled, but didn't reach out for it. I speculated idly what it would look like in the water, but really, I was too comfortable to bother checking.

Mickie returned and said, in an upward inflection, "Sam's turn?"

My turn for what? I wondered.

"She better have a good sense of direction," Mickie muttered.

It should've annoyed me that she spoke about me like I wasn't there, but I felt so perfectly content that I just ignored her. Will frowned my direction, his index finger gliding to his lips as if to confirm I should disregard his sister. *Fine by me,* I thought.

"Sam's good," Will said. He set another rock by my first two.

I smiled at him and then turned my gaze to the new stone. It was pinker than the others. It would look beautiful if it got wet. I reached for the stone. My hand didn't seem to follow my volition, though. *Odd*, I thought, bending my gaze towards my arm.

Then several things happened at almost the same moment. I realized I couldn't see my arm. Will reached out as if to touch me and out of nowhere, like someone started a movie in my head, I saw a crisp image—a dark-featured girl with her hands on her hips. She looked thirteen or fourteen, and she sure seemed angry. She pointed, shouting, towards a receding ambulance. I couldn't hear what she said.

The image faded, I solidified, and Mickie shrieked.

5

INSUBSTANTIAL

For a moment we sat without words as Mickie processed what her eyes had just registered.

"Impossible," she whispered. Then, her voice low and icy, she asked, "What have you done, Will?"

"Nothing."

"She can *ripple* Will." Her tone was venomous.

"Yeah, no kidding?" He continued sorting rocks.

Angry fire danced in her eyes and I was grateful it was directed at her brother. "You swore, Will. You swore an oath on our mother's grave."

I didn't know people still did that.

"You're making an assumption without checking your facts," Will said.

"The hell I am! I just saw her ripple, and you don't so much as blink an eye? I think I have all the evidence I need to understand what's going on here."

"I didn't tell her."

"Oh, she just figured out you have Rippler's Syndrome all by herself?" Mickie asked. "Oh, I get it. You didn't tell her. You showed her. That's still breaking your promise. God, Will, what were you thinking?"

I stared from Will to Mick and back again. Will had Rippler's Syndrome? And he hadn't let on?

Furious, I shouted, "Why didn't you tell me?" and Will, at almost the same time, shouted at his sister, "I said I didn't tell her and I meant it. But you just took care of that, didn't you?"

"What?" Mickie and I asked the question together.

Both siblings ignored me.

Will's dark gaze matched his sister's. "You heard me the first time."

Shock registered on Mickie's face. It looked like Will was the only person not getting a major reveal today, because if I understood right, Will had the same condition I did, only he'd kept it a secret from me because of an oath his sister had forced him to swear on their dead mom's grave. Except now, she'd blown it.

Will spoke. "This has nothing to do with you, Mickie."

"Nothing to do with me? This has everything to do with me. You're my responsibility!"

"I don't *need* you to take care of me, Mick. I'm not a

54

child anymore."

"When are you going to grow up, Will?"

They were both silent. I spoke quietly, "I can't believe you didn't tell me."

"I made a promise," he said.

Mickie continued as though I hadn't spoken. "I made a promise, Will: I told Mom I'd watch out for you!" Her voice was tight and pinched, but she refused to give in to tears. "How am I supposed to take care of you if you can't even keep this a secret?"

"I'm not the one who let the cat out of the bag, Mick. And believe me, Sam's perfectly aware of what could happen if someone finds out."

"You've *told* her what could happen? Oh, that's just great." She threw her hands up. "Great. You never think through the consequences of your actions, do you?"

"I trust her," Will said, his voice quiet and tense.

"Well, that's a damn good thing, isn't it? Seeing as how she's holding our lives in her hands at this moment." Mickie struggled to maintain her composure, face pale with anger.

Will's gaze was cold and hard, unfathomable.

Then Mickie spoke softly. "You need to recognize there are consequences for every action you take, Will."

"Maybe I'm sick and tired of us *not* taking action," Will said.

"Do you *want* people to find you? Who should we

tell first? Do you want the experimental physicists to know? The CIA? How about the mystery assassins who took out Pfeffer? Our dad maybe? There's an idea— Dad could just sell you to the highest bidder."

Will exploded. "Give it a friggin' rest, Mick!"

Mickie sat frozen, gazing unseeing across the creek. "I need some time. Meet me at the car in an hour."

She stood up and marched off leaving me alone with Will, not even collecting her pack, but I wasn't about to call after her.

Will and I sat without speaking: Will staring at the creek, me staring at Will. He picked up and skipped a rock. It glanced elegantly across the glassy surface, curving off to the right and clattering onto the rocky shore opposite.

"I didn't mean for you to hear it like this," he said gruffly. He chose another flat stone, aimed it across the smooth, wet plane. "I wanted to tell you all along."

I felt a lot of ways right now, but "hurt" topped the list. "I can't believe you never said anything to me."

Will continued skipping rocks until he exhausted his supply. He looked around half-heartedly for more, then gave that up as well and lay back with a sigh. "Look, I'm sorry. About not telling you. Really, really sorry. But it's like you heard. Mick made me swear on my mom's grave that I wouldn't tell *anyone*."

I kicked my heel against the loose granite-gravel, then nodded. "I get that."

He sat up again, elbows on knees, palms grinding into his forehead. "You must be wishing you'd stayed in Las Abs."

"No," I said. "It's beautiful here. I'm glad I came."

He lowered his palms from his head. His eyes, hidden under the fringe of lashes, slowly rose until he met my gaze. He smiled a sad, half-smile. "Well, that's one good thing out of this whole mess."

"And I'm glad I know. About you," I said, still holding his eyes with mine.

"Yeah." He sighed and his shoulders relaxed several inches. "It'll be a lot easier to teach you how to control what you're doing now I don't have to keep my knowledge a secret."

"That'll be great."

"That leaves us with one important question," he said, eyes sober and fixed on mine.

I straightened up, ready for anything.

"Your step-mom," he said. "How's her cheesecake?"

I laughed. "It's the best." I reached in my pack and cut him a slice.

"Looks great. Forks?"

I rummaged through my pack for a minute before remembering I'd left the forks on the counter at home. "Oops."

Will shrugged, picked up the whole piece, and stuffed half of it in his mouth. His eyes widened. "It'th delithouth!"

I laughed. "I'll tell her you said so. Exactly like that."

Will finished chewing and swallowed before adding, "Nice of Mick to take off. More for us." He held out a hand for seconds.

I frowned. It was my fault Mickie had taken off.

"Don't even *think* about feeling bad. Mick's like a volcano. She's not happy unless she lets off steam every couple days." Will shook his head. "Seriously, it's her problem, not yours. It's not like you did it on purpose." He looked inquisitively at me. "*Did* you disappear on purpose?"

I shook my head no. "I only noticed when I went to grab this rock and I couldn't see my arm." I held up the pinkish rock. "So, does stuff disappear if you pick it up when you're invisible, or does it just sort of hover out in the air?"

"Neither."

"Either you can see it or you can't."

"No, it's not like that—you can't pick things up once you ripple."

"Huh?" I stared at him, feeling confused. "Why not?"

"Wow, Sam, it's weird you haven't noticed this— no offense—it's just that there isn't any 'you' to pick something up with, you know?" He paused. "I mean, I guess it isn't *that* weird, you not noticing. You haven't rippled much."

"Are you saying I don't have any . . . substance? When I ripple I'm not just invisible, I'm . . ." I broke off, not able to figure out what the opposite of having substance would be.

"Mickie used to get so mad at me for rippling when we were little. She'd have us playing tea party or Barbies or something and I'd get bored. If I would try to run away, she would catch me. But if I rippled, she couldn't grab me or figure out where I was. She tried a lot before she figured out it didn't work. She said that the air got really cold where I rippled, though, so sometimes she could tell I was still in the room, and she'd bribe me to come back and play."

I laughed, picturing Will being forced to play dolls with his sister.

"You tell anyone about the Barbies and you're toast," he said, grinning.

"So, where does your body 'go' when you ripple?"

"No idea."

"Creepy. So, it's a good thing that I know how to come back, then."

Will nodded, fingering the pink rock I had set down. "When I was little, I'd see something and want it, and if I was invisible, I couldn't grab it. I remember that really pissed me off."

"There go my plans to decimate the Merced Mall."

He looked over at me to see if I was serious.

"I'm joking."

"It would appeal to plenty of people. My dad, for instance. Mickie wasn't stretching it when she said he'd sell me to the highest bidder. Or sell you. He's never cared about anything but his next fix. Least, since I've been alive." Will nudged a couple of large rocks into the creek with his foot. "Mom died thanks to his habit."

I thought Will had said breast cancer, but I didn't want to bring up things he might not want to talk about. I had led a sheltered existence compared to Will. I had parents, normal parents, who actually loved me; Will only had Mickie.

He stood and repositioned himself at the edge of the creek, squatting. I couldn't see his face. He doused his hands, face, and hair.

"Hoooo-eeee," he hollered, "that's some cold water." He turned and grinned at me.

I smiled back and then gazed at the golden creek once more. The surging water would plunge over Illilouette Fall then join the Merced River where Will had first seen me vanish. All at once it hit me: There'd been *water* each of the times I'd disappeared.

"Will! It's water! Water is what makes me vanish."
"Huh?"

"Get this, Will: I *love* water. It completely relaxes me to stare at a river or lake or, well, anything with water." Suddenly I saw a flash from the day we buried Mom; I'd held it together staring at falling snow and icicles all day. Goosebumps ran along my arms as I realized something else that had happened that day— something I just realized. *I'd rippled.*

"Huh," Will grunted. "Water. That's different."

"How do you ripple?" I asked.

"Me? Oh, uh . . . hmmm . . ." His eyes took on a glazed-over, far-away look. "I kind of go inside myself, to a space where it's really calm and peaceful. Then I'm gone."

Could I learn to do that? Instead of staring at water? Not that I wanted to do this more often.

Will interrupted my thoughts. "If water calms you, that makes sense. Have you always found water soothing?"

"As far back as I can remember. Dad says Mom called me her water-baby."

"Huh," said Will. "I wonder why you didn't ripple more when you were . . . you know . . . before your Mom passed."

I hesitated a second but decided to tell him what I'd just figured out. "The day we buried Mom, I must have rippled; people said they couldn't find me. There were icicles hanging from the eaves by my bedroom window seat. I watched drops slide down the spokes and hang a moment before freezing. It was like the house cried for Mom. Those icicles, they were like these pure, perfect things.

"I heard people talking about me, downstairs. How

resourceful I'd been calling 9-1-1, how brave I was. Which was a bunch of crap. Maybe shell-shocked and brave look the same to adults. I mean, I hadn't cried. Not since the ambulance came to take Maggie and my mom away. But that didn't mean I felt brave. Just . . . anesthetized."

Will sat silent. My eyes blurred and I realized I was crying. Will didn't judge or comment. I kept talking.

"I sat there all day looking out my window and never got cold or hungry. I remember lunch-smells creeping up the stairs and then coffee smells. A woman carried cocoa to my room, and I heard her call my name, but I didn't turn. I just kept looking out my window at the snow falling and the ice melting, and she left.

"And when it was time for the burial, my cousin ran into my room, checked my closet, pulled the duvet off my bed, and thumped out, shouting I wasn't in my room. I ignored him. But then my dad started calling my name, and he sounded worried. I must have come solid then; Dad saw me. And here's a weird thing I remember. When I turned to my Dad's voice, I finally felt the cold. It was like a wall of *ice* shattering on me."

"Temperature change," Will said. "It's the biggest clue you get when you ripple. You can't feel the outside temperature. Or hunger. Or thirst. Until you return solid."

I nodded. "I wanted to tell Dad I wasn't going, but

my teeth chattered so bad I literally couldn't talk." *So I let them bundle me into layers. I let them buckle me into the car. I let them lower her into the ground: a dark wound in the deathly white.*

Will didn't tell me he was sorry or any of the other lame-ass things people say.

I blinked back tears and spoke again. "Before your sister found out about me, just now, I was completely chilled, watching the creek. When I realized I'd rippled, I panicked and came solid. At least I think that's what happened."

"You left your ripple-zone. You were startled. Your dad calling for you would've done that, if you weren't focusing on staying immaterial."

"I'm gonna test out my water-theory." I turned to face the creek. "And you can see if it's cold where I am . . . or was . . . or whatever."

"I already did," said Will, looking a bit sheepish. "I ran my hand through you—through where I thought you were—right before Mount Saint Mickie erupted. It felt ice-cold."

I smiled at the moniker he'd given his sister. "Well," I said, "Here goes . . ."

I gazed at the creek. The sun was heading west, toward the cliff we had descended earlier. Light, filtering through pines and laurels, flickered on the water. I relaxed as I saw bright and dark dancing along the creek, casting shadows on granite rocks below the surface.

There were pine needles stuck between some of the rocks. They were dark, rusty-brown, with five needles each, which I thought meant sugar pine, one needle for each letter in *sugar*.

Was I invisible? I closed my eyes, took a slow breath, and shifted my gaze so that when I opened my eyes I would see, or not see, my knees. My eyes opened.

I was gone.

I smiled. Thought a smile, anyway. *I have no lips to smile with. That is seriously creepy . . .* I thought of turning and found myself facing Will. He wore an enormous grin. He brushed his hand 'through' me and laughed. As his hand passed through me, my vision shifted and for the second time it felt as if I were looking at a movie; I saw a beautiful girl, smiling and sitting by the creek eating cheesecake. I realized with a shock that the girl was me. Then my vision corrected itself and I was looking at Will again. I'd have to ask him why I kept seeing movies.

I turned away from Will's grinning face to the creek. Then I realized, if I could turn my head, I could probably walk. I'd never thought of trying to move; I'd assumed I was "stuck," in fact. I looked at a large boulder in the creek and launched myself towards it. Magical! I felt as if I were a kayak cutting through a still lake, with nothing resisting my passage. The creek burbled past the place where my legs should be—rather, where my legs *were*—it was no use pretending I didn't have a strong sense that I still *existed* somehow. In fact, I had never felt so piercingly alive.

I couldn't sense the icy cold of the creek. I felt perfect temperature-wise. But I could make out a whisper of feeling as I passed through the water or as it passed through me. It was like when I ran by the willows, arms outstretched. *Like dry water!* I focused my thought upon the sensation and it increased from a whisper to a shiver.

I needed to solidify to ask a million questions. I turned to face Will and, still standing within the creek, I rippled back.

An explosive crackling, like thunder, left my ears ringing. Something had gone wrong. Will's alarmed expression mirrored my own. I stood in ice-cold water up to my shins while a downpour struck against me from all sides. Then the force of the river asserted itself against my legs. It felt furious, strong, and I threw my arms out to maintain my balance. Will closed the span between us with an arm to catch me back from the angry water.

For a moment I was safe.

Then I slipped and lost Will's hand, and the raging creek carried me downstream. Instinctively I shielded my head with my arms as I shot down, feet first. Last winter's heavy snow-pack meant the water flowed swiftly. I couldn't regain my footing, but I hoped I might be able to grab a tree limb as I shot beneath the snag. I reached and missed, the water plunging me under. Icy-cold gripped like a giant hand squeezing air from my lungs.

I bobbed to the surface again, choking on the freezing water. I grabbed at boulders as I raced past them, but it was hopeless. The rocks were slippery; I was slippery. And suddenly I was terrified.

If I couldn't stop myself, I would plunge over the falls. *I want to live;* the thought resounded in my head. Forgetting about protecting my head, I flailed, trying to catch hold of something, anything, as I careened with the icy flow.

A group of boulders loomed large ahead, forcing the creek to narrow and surge between the solid masses. Something to grab hold of, or be smashed senseless upon. My arms flew to my head again, but water forced its way into my nostrils, down to my lungs, and as I choked, I lost any hope of catching myself against the boulders. I couldn't breathe. *No!* I was going to be thrown onto the rocks and my broken body would ride over the falls to the Merced River. I coughed furiously, cleared my airway, and tried to see as I hurtled into the stone wall.

6

IMPACT

I slammed into the wall: it hurt less than I'd expected. Was I too numbed by the cold water to feel things properly? It seemed as if my body pushed against the current. My eyes opened and, looking down at my waist, I saw strong arms wrapped tightly around me. Will!

He inched us along the boulder to shore, slipping once, but catching himself. I was too exhausted to speak, too numb from cold to help.

"Thank God," Will sighed low, hugging me to himself.

I felt the warmth of his body pressed into mine. I tried to hug back, but my frozen arms didn't respond. My head nestled in the space below his chin, and I breathed his scent of peanut-butter sandwich and pine and sweat. We collapsed on dry land, slipping apart, avoiding eye contact, embarrassed.

I shook from cold or from remembering the shape of Will's arms around me.

"You're bleeding," Will said, pointing to my elbow—a bloody gash.

It stung as I thawed.

"Firs-taid-tsin-mupack." My lungs and nostrils burned and my words slurred. I turned my head coughing out creek-water.

"I'm not leaving you here for Band-Aids."

I lifted my leaden arm to examine my elbow. It was an ugly scrape.

Will reached beyond me and placed something he'd grabbed onto the cut. I winced briefly.

"Wuz-zat?" I asked.

"Cobweb," he replied. "Stops small injuries from bleeding."

"Nuh-uh." I laughed, more like a snort. "Where-d-chu-hear-that?"

"Shakespeare."

I coughed, my throat stinging. Feeling was returning to my mouth and jaw muscles. "You're *such* a history geek." My words had returned.

Will shook his head grimly; his dark eyes were serious. "All I could think was I had to catch you before the falls. I remembered this spot where the boulders almost touch."

It made no sense that he could outrun the river, not with all the brush, fallen trees and uneven rocks surrounding the creek. "How did you get here so fast?"

"I rippled."

I recalled the friction-free movement. "You can move faster invisible."

"Well, yeah, if you glide straight through all the rocks and stuff."

"Um—wait a sec—you passed *through* things?" I felt dizzy.

He shrugged like it was no big deal for him.

I thought for a moment. "Guess I just 'passed through' water."

He nodded. "So, Sam, just now, when you rippled back solid upstream—what happened? I was watching for you and all the sudden there's this thunderclap and water flying everywhere and you in the middle of it all in the creek."

I shook my head. "You're the expert. Does an explosion happen like that every time you materialize in water?"

Will shook his head. "I've never done what you did."

I didn't like the idea that Will was as new to this as I was, but all I said was, "Huh."

So materializing in a creek was apparently not a good idea. My mind looked for explanations, for answers. When I vanished into thin air, what happened?

The air shimmered. "Will, what if I did that—the explosion. What if my body displaced the water? You say the air ripples, right? Maybe the air shimmers like that because it's being disrupted somehow."

"Maybe. Although, if that's true, it's more dramatic in water than in air." Will frowned. "What would happen the other direction? If you rippled *invisible* while standing in water?"

"You wouldn't be displacing anything. Water would just rush in to fill the space," I said, guessing.

"Probably," Will said. "Congratulations, by the way."

"For what?"

"For rippling on purpose. Although, the coming back was a bit drama-queen."

I dropped a hand into the creek and splashed Will.

"Hey, what was that for?" he asked, spluttering.

"I almost die and you call me a drama queen?"

Will tried to look serious, but his mouth curved up on one side.

"Going over a waterfall is NOT funny," I said.

"*Very* not funny."

My own mouth quirked at the corners.

"Splat," said Will.

We both exploded into giggles, laughing and shaking, gasping for breath. Every time we tried to stop, one of us said "splat!" and we'd be off again. At last we lay back on the gravel shore, smiling pathetically at one another.

Suddenly I wanted to kiss that smiling mouth, taste the little tears that had squeezed out of the corners of his eyes. I swallowed hard. *You don't need complicated right now. Look away.* I tried, but my eyes drifted back. Will's lips: soft, full—what would they feel like touching mine?

Will groaned, sitting up. "We should start back."

I stood, shaky at first. Will reached out an arm to support me, and I practiced *not* thinking about him holding me again, rooting around in my brain for something *else* to focus on. I had a few things, fortunately.

"You've been seriously holding out about how *cool* it is, gliding around invisible," I said.

"Yeah. Well, something about a blood oath and a temperamental sister."

"That feeling, though . . . I don't even know the words . . . I need a new vocabulary. That sensation of water rushing *through* your legs when you're invisible: how do you begin to describe that?"

He frowned. "I've never paid attention to water flowing through me. But I know what you're getting at. I *love* walking through walls."

"I can walk *through walls?*"

"It's awesome! And they all feel different. Stone walls are amazing—the best. Cement and cinder block walls are a bit, I don't know, screechy or something. You'll see what I mean. And windows are seriously

71

trippy. I won't even try to describe that feeling." He grinned like a kid showing off a missing-tooth.

"I want to try it!" I enthused. "All of it!" Any resentment, any fears, any frustration with being a 'freak' fell off me like a shed skin. What I could do was *wonderful*—why hadn't I recognized this before?

"Do you have any idea how cool it will be to share this stuff with someone?" Will shook his head, looking dazedly happy. "I used to try to describe things to Mick when we were little, but she'd get sullen and walk away. I haven't tried for years." He ruffled his hair with his fingers. "Hey, Sam, up top at Glacier Point, there's this stone shelter, for looking out at the different points of interest. You want to find out what it feels like to pass through a rock wall?"

I did, but I was worried—what if there were people around? What if I solidified at the wrong moment?

He must have seen the conflict in my eyes. "Only if there's no one around—I guess we don't know how well you'll be able to control your ripple yet, huh?"

As it turned out, when we arrived people were swarming all over Glacier Point, so no rock walls for us. And no Mickie, either. We found a note she had placed under the windshield wiper:

Will, I caught a ride with a friend I ran into. You have my keys assuming you grabbed my pack. Wreck my Jeep and you're dead. Mick. P.S. Make a donation to the trail fund. You've got my wallet. P.P. S. If you forgot my pack, go back and get it

NOW. You're dead if you left it there.

He sent gravel flying with an angry kick. "Forget her. We're getting ice cream." He turned and began walking back to the snack bar.

I hesitated and he looked behind to see why I wasn't with him.

"I didn't bring any money," I said.

Will laughed, unzipped a pocket of his sister's pack, and pulled out her wallet, waving it in the air. "Mick's buying."

A few minutes later we sank our teeth into Toll House Cookie ice-cream-sandwich-Nirvana. Will popped the change from his sister's twenty into the Yosemite Trail Fund box.

Will finished before I did and started digging through his pack. "Look." He held up the small black book of riddles, waving it gleefully. A couple of tourists looked over at him as they moved past in a line. "Let's drive up the road—it's kind of crowded here," murmured Will.

I knew he must be putting off seeing his sister. I was happy to be the person he preferred. We drove the switchbacks out of the parking lot and a mile later, Will turned off for Washburn Point. Another view to make you forget to breathe.

"You can't see Yosemite Valley from here," Will said apologetically.

"I don't miss it," I whispered. I felt suspended on

top of the world, dangling aloft over one of its edges.

Will smiled. "Come on." He scrambled up a large boulder, sat, and pulled open his sister's pack. He thumped a section of rock next to him. "Sit close and we won't have to talk loud."

I scooted to where I could feel his breath, warm on my bare shoulder.

A chipmunk joined us on the boulder, inquisitive. Will flipped through the book, looking for additional sections with English translations. The chipmunk turned its head to one side and made a dash to retrieve a bit of potato chip by Will's feet.

"I see words that remind me of Spanish or French," he said.

I nodded in agreement. "Some of this looks like Latin. Maybe we should try a translating program online?"

"We could try Latin-to-English and see what comes up."

"Wait," I said. "Flip back a couple pages. There." I pointed at the small neat handwriting—another English translation.

Leaning our heads together, we read:

In a dark, cold room, three boys with eager fists approach three other boys.

"Give us your blankets," says the largest boy, Hans.

The smallest, Wolfi, is clever but not strong, and he passes his blanket to Hans. "It is scratchy. And it smells of rotten vegetables. Take it."

Hans sniffs the blanket, discovering the small boy has told the truth. He drops the coverlet to the ground. "Give me yours," Hans demands of another of the boys—the one with brown eyes.

"I'm sharing with Karl and Wolfi," replies the brown-eyed boy. He stands his ground, although he is afraid. "You find someone else to share with."

Hans shrugs and turns as if to concede. Then, as a smile warms the brown eyes, Hans turns suddenly, delivering a savage kick to the stomach.

"Pepper!" cry Karl and Wolfi.

Hans grabs the blanket as Pepper struggles for breath.

The translation ended and I stopped reading, looking up. The beauty of the Sierra Nevada spread about us no longer spoke to me. I felt sick.

"It's like the scratchy-blanket thing really happened," said Will. "Assuming this is someone's journal."

I nodded.

"You okay?" asked Will.

"This book isn't just a journal: it's someone's experiments written down. What if the other ones happened too? About the food and the poison? It's revolting."

"A twisted experiment in Eugenics and Behaviorism." Will gazed out over the Sierra. "Survival of the fittest. What do you want to bet this was Germany in the 1930's?"

"It's not written in German," I pointed out.

A tourist bus pulled in, brakes squealing. The chipmunks fled our boulder.

"Time to go?" asked Will.

"Yeah," I said.

I felt shaky as I stood. Will offered to help me down off the boulder, and I took his hand in mine. It felt callused but warm.

I couldn't let go.

Will smiled, gave my hand a quick squeeze and released it, fishing his sister's keys from a pocket. His very *angry* sister's keys. Would she take him away from Las Abuelitas?

I couldn't let him go.

"Do you think your sister's packing up your place right now?"

He frowned. "The thing is, if Mick's curious enough about you, she won't want to leave. She's got scientific curiosity, but she's paranoid. She could go either way."

I felt cold stealing across my neck and shoulders in the warm evening. "It's my fault. I don't want you guys to move."

"Yeah," Will said, opening my door.

Yeah, it was my fault or *yeah*, he didn't want to move either?

He started the engine. "Man, I am starving. Pizza Factory in Oakhurst? Mick's buying."

I nodded, grinning. I could always pay her back later. If she'd speak to me. If they stayed. I shoved the thoughts away.

At Pizza Factory, we talked about cross country, classes, the French Club's trip to Europe in December. We didn't talk about packing or Will's sister. We didn't talk about saying goodbye.

We arrived back at my house as the stars were popping out. At my doorway, Will brushed a hair off my face, lightly. Neither of us spoke, and then he was gone.

I should have fallen asleep as soon as I crawled in bed, what with an exhausting hike, a near-death experience and a belly full of pizza. But my mind refused to shut down.

Will is just like me.

How crazy was that? Will couldn't leave town. I couldn't lose him.

I had to keep him here.

I jumped out of bed, shoved my legs into the first pair of jeans I found and pulled a hoodie over my nightshirt. This couldn't wait until tomorrow. I had to sneak out of the house.

I smiled because all I needed to sneak out of the house was a little running water.

Sylvia did my bathroom like those magazines with bathroom-as-artwork on the back cover. And right now, what I needed was to run some water out of my artsy faucet into my artsy basin.

I flicked on the lights and started the water. Sitting on the edge of my tub, I gazed at the cylinder of moving liquid, but the florescent lighting overhead didn't exactly cast the room in an inspiring glow.

I rummaged through a drawer of scrunchies and cotton balls and found what I needed. Striking a match, I lit two votives, one on either side of the sink. Then I flicked off the fluorescents.

The column of water descended noiselessly into the basin, and with a luminary on either side, the water seemed to catch fire, pulsing and glowing with each flare and gutter of the burning candles.

I thought about all that water running while I was gone, probably breaking fourteen California laws on conservation. I stood to plug the drain and turn off the water. The water in the basin shimmered in the candlelight.

It was magical. Elemental. A dance of fire and water.

I caught a ripple passing across the mirror behind the sink and looked up to see myself fade.

Weird.

I glided downstairs, past my dad and Sylvia. They tidied the kitchen while discussing me and Will. I wanted to hear the conversation, but I wanted to get to Will more. Dad opened the sliding glass door, and I dashed outside, relieved I didn't have to try walking through walls at the moment.

Passing invisibly down the dilapidated highway towards Will's house, I saw pairs of nocturnal eyes flicker my direction before taking flight. Did they sense a disturbance as I passed? I laughed. Without a mouth. Strange—no wonder animals ran from me.

As I neared the Baker's cabin, I began to have second thoughts about knocking on their door. They could be sleeping. They could be packing. And how the heck was I planning to force them to stay? The thought of Mickie's temper made me want to run back home.

I saw lights on inside and heard voices in the yard out back. I ghosted behind the old house and saw Mickie, standing where the houselights cast a glow upon her. She glared at her younger brother. I pulled back into the shadows, all thoughts of rematerializing gone for the moment.

Gazing past the siblings into the cottage-sized dwelling, I saw stacked boxes. They were moving. I felt a deep ache inside, even without a body.

"I won't go," Will said. He was turned from me, but I could imagine the stubborn expression playing across his face.

"You damned well aren't staying," Mick replied.

"I'm eighteen. You can't force me to go anywhere. Not if I don't want to."

"Is this about her?"

"That's none of your business."

My heart squeezed.

"You know how complicated our lives are right now," said Mickie. "This is not the time—it wouldn't be fair to her."

"I'm not having this conversation with you. Even if there *were* anything to talk about."

Mickie let loose a string of highly uncomplimentary adjectives ending with the word "idiot."

Neither spoke for over a minute.

"Aw, Mick, don't." Will moved closer to his sister. "Don't cry."

She was crying?

"Listen." He spoke gently. "There's been no sign that we're being tracked. It's been almost two years since the Pfeffer disappeared. Maybe we're safe now, Mick."

Mickie sat down on a large log. She drew in a long and shaky breath. Will sat down beside her and cautiously put one arm over her shoulder.

"There's something I haven't told you," Mickie said, her voice flat, dull. "Three researchers who studied Helmann's Disease just died from a gas leak. They studied *Helmann's*, Will; not even Rippler's Syndrome. Things are escalating."

7

OVERHEARD

A shiver ran along my spine. It took me a moment to realize what that meant—that I had a solid spine again. The shadows hid me as I listened.

"I read it in the Fresno Bee. Two days ago. I didn't know how to tell you or what we should do about it. I hoped time hiking in the Park would help me clear my mind." Mickie sniffled, passing the back of her hand across her nose. "And I wanted to give you a nice memory to keep of your new friend. Will, I was thinking about moving already, even before finding out there's another rippler in this town."

"How do you know they were killed? Did the paper say it was murder?"

"Will, come on. *Gas leaks?* It's like whoever's behind this isn't even worried about covering their tracks."

"You're telling me the truth, Mick? This isn't some crazy way to get me in the Jeep right now?"

"Like I'd make this stuff up?"

"You *hid* this from me."

"I hid it so the news wouldn't wreck your trip to Yosemite."

Will hurled a rock far into the dark night. "Geez, Mick, when are you going to stop treating me like a kid?"

She put her head in her hands, elbows resting on her knees.

Will sighed heavily and looked at his sister. "Aw, crap. I'm sorry. I know you'd do anything to keep me safe."

"Not lie to you, idiot."

"Yeah. Okay. I said sorry."

Mickie shambled to one of her garden beds and began pulling weeds, something I'd seen Sylvia do when she was stressed.

"Maybe there really was a gas leak, but it wasn't intentional," said Will.

"Not intentional?" Mick hurled a large weed past the cabin. "You know that's bullsh—"

Her expletive was drowned by my yelp of pain as my eyes closed too late, trapping dirt missiles between my eyeballs and eyelids.

Will was at my side immediately, herding me

towards the kitchen. I heard Mickie shuffling in behind us, heard her open the refrigerator.

"Milk works better," she said.

The water Will guided over my eyes had already removed the dirt, but not the scratchy feeling. Mickie moved her brother, held my head in one hand, and slowly poured milk over my eyes. The relief was amazing.

"Thanks." I sneezed as milk ran up my nose.

"A towel, here, Will?" Mickie's voice had a defeated edge.

"Where'd you learn that? About milk?" I asked.

"Raising this idiot," Mick mumbled, passing me a towel.

I dabbed at milk, tears, mud, and a bit of leftover mascara draining from my eyes. Glamorous.

"Didn't see you there hiding in the dark," said Mickie.

I couldn't tell if her remark was an apology or an accusation.

"'S'okay," I mumbled beneath the towel.

"What did you hear out there?" Will asked me.

Mickie muttered, "Oh, here we go," and collapsed on an ancient papasan chair, cradling her head in her hands.

"Something about dead people who studied Helmann's," I replied.

"It's past your curfew," Will said. "Did you ripple

to come over here?"

I nodded, a proud smile spreading across my face. I wanted to whisper to Will how amazing it was, gliding through the night like a shadow, but seeing his sister, I wiped the grin off my face.

Will turned to Mickie. "There's one option you haven't considered, yet."

She looked up at him wearily, across a row of boxes filled with books and kitchen pots. "Killing you myself so I don't have to worry about someone else beating me to it?"

Will laughed.

His sister scowled.

"Mick, you've finally met someone who can ripple," Will said. "Besides me, obviously. Just think about how much more there is to learn here. Not to mention, your objectivity would be a million percent if you didn't have to rely on me for all your info on rippling."

"There's no such thing as a million percent. I swear I'm homeschooling you next year." Mickie growled and I realized what she reminded me of: a mama bear with a cub. She would do whatever it took to keep Will safe.

"Aren't you curious?" Will asked. "Knowledge is power, man."

Mickie looked from me to her brother, frustration and desire mixing equally on her face. "Yeah, well who taught you that?"

She wanted to know more about me.

"I'd be honored to be part of your research," I said.

"I'll sleep on it," Mickie said. She rose and walked down a short hall and kicked open what had to be her bedroom door.

"Her door sticks bad," Will muttered.

Will insisted on walking me home. The jeep would have drawn attention to the fact I was breaking curfew, and he wasn't having me go by myself, which I told him was nice but a bit pointless. I could've just rippled again and kept perfectly safe.

He shrugged and smiled. "Maybe I like your company better than my sister's at the moment."

My heart squeezed. "I was afraid you'd be packing up," I whispered. "I came over to check."

"We were packing. Well, my sister was," he said. "But I don't think she'll go through with it. Not after the way we both played the knowledge card on her." He laughed. "You were brilliant! 'I'd be honored?' Genius!"

"I *would* be honored, dweeb," I said, elbowing his ribs.

He chortled. "Okay, okay. So I'll text you tomorrow morning."

"You're sure you won't be leaving?" I asked.

"I'm starting school on Monday," he said. "With or without Mick."

"See you Monday," I said.

Will took off at a run into the weird glow of fog

visibility lights. The warm night air rippled around him and he was gone.

When I awoke the next morning, Sunday, I had two text messages: one each from Will and Gwyn.

"i know micks curiosity will get the best of her c u monday"

I sent a smiley face to Will and flipped to Gwyn's message.

"ok sam spill the beans how was yosemite i heard u came back alone i mean w/o his sister!!! i m gettin kittens in Oakhurst. come with! tell me everything!!!"

I pointed out she couldn't legally drive me.

"hello! tell your folks i m 17," she replied.

My folks didn't ask, and within an hour Gwyn and I were humming down the road in her mom's Mini Cooper. Before we left my driveway, she started the cross-examination.

"So, Yosemite? Tell me everything. The whole town says you came back with just Will last night."

I rolled my eyes. "Why would the whole town even care?"

"Um, well, in case you hadn't noticed, there's a distinct lack of entertainment options here."

Sam as entertainment? This was new. I tried to figure out what I could reveal, what I had to hide. "They had a fight," I finally said. "And she took off and we were supposed to meet up at the car, but then she left a note saying she'd gotten her own ride home."

"Wow. Fighting with your sibling takes on a whole different dimension when there's no Mom or Dad to force you to get along."

"Yeah," I agreed. "They get along pretty well. I think Mickie has kind of a short fuse, though."

"Bet she gets that from her bad-dad," Gwyn said.

"Probably."

"So, I asked Ma about Will." She looked at me anxiously. "How much do you like him?"

My smile gave me away.

"Uh-oh," she said.

"What do you mean, 'uh-oh'?" I demanded.

"I'm not sure you're going to like what I have to tell you."

"So stop being dramatic and just spit it out."

She lowered her sunglasses 'til they rested on the tip of her nose and then looked imperiously over the top of them at me. "*Moi?* Dramatic? Please."

I sighed. She was impossible to hurry in this mood.

"So you know how Ma has all these rental properties?" asked Gwyn.

"No," I said. "I thought she just owned the bakery building."

"Yeah, that and about a dozen others," said Gwyn, taking a curve fifteen miles-an-hour over the speed limit.

My eyebrows leapt up. "Really? No offense, but you guys don't exactly live like real estate tycoons. And what does this have to do with Will?"

"I'm getting there," Gwyn said. "And you're right. The living-simple is this totally Chinese thing: you work your ass off so your kids can get ahead." Gwyn rolled her eyes dramatically.

"That sounds nice," I said, wondering how I'd get us back to Will again.

"Yeah, Ma has this plan I'm going to be a doctor so she's saving for med school. Which I'm totally not doing. I'm moving to Hawaii and opening a yogurt stand. You can work there for me if you want."

I chuckled. "Okay, Gwyn. Just cut to the chase and tell me this bad stuff your mom told you about Will."

"Fine." She paused. "So here's the thing: Will and Mickie rent from Ma, and their rent is paid every month from one of those tiny countries in Europe that have banks people use to hide their money because it's illegally acquired or dirty somehow. Slovakia. No. Sweden, maybe?"

"Do you mean Switzerland?" I asked.

"That's the one," she said, red lips pinching together. "Switzerland. So anyways, some nefarious criminal pays their rent every month."

I frowned. "I don't think having a Swiss bank account makes you automatically a criminal, Gwyn."

She shrugged. "Or maybe their dad makes big money selling drugs and they know all about it but they turn a blind eye."

"Or maybe their mom wanted to prevent their dad from ever accessing her kids' money," I said. "Honestly, Gwyn, just because you can make up a crazy story doesn't mean it's true."

"Maybe. But Ma says they're a strange pair."

"This, from the woman who thinks *you* want to be a doctor?"

She laughed so hard she snorted. "Yeah, maybe you're right."

"I'm just saying, this is Will Baker we're talking about. Politest-guy-on-the-planet-Will. And Sylvia really likes his sister."

"I know," said Gwyn, sighing. "But I care about you. And there's just something about them that doesn't add up. That's all I'm saying. So be careful."

I gazed out at the pines flashing past and wondered if there was anything I could say without giving away their secrets. Finally I said something about how they'd both been through a lot, and didn't everyone deserve a second chance?

"Now you sound like Ma," said Gwyn. "Please. I get enough of the bleeding heart club at home. Maybe some people deserve a second chance, but I think it all depends on what they did with their first chance."

I sensed this was an argument I couldn't win.

"But I'll give you cute," she said, grinning mischievously. "He's all over tall, dark, and handsome."

I smiled.

"Maybe he's bi-polar, you know, like Jekyll and Hyde," said Gwyn.

I shook my head. "I don't think being bi-polar was Hyde's problem. Not to mention, it's fiction."

"Truth is stranger than fiction, girlfriend," said Gwyn, looking at me over the top of her sunglasses again.

You have no idea, I thought.

"Does he *like* you?" Gwyn asked.

She slowed for a hairpin curve and a pair of dragonflies whirred past, their white tails a sharp contrast to their black-and-clear wings. I couldn't tell if they were flying with or away from one another.

"Maybe," I said. "I don't know. It's complicated. He might not want to . . . think of me that way, even if he does like me. His sister's got this no-dating thing."

"You like him."

"I want to be his friend."

"Liar, liar, pumpkin-eater!"

I cracked up. "Liar, liar, *pumpkin eater?*"

"Pants-on-fire. Whatever. Quit laughing at me or I'm taking you home right now."

I laughed harder.

"The only reason you are in this car is because I felt sorry for you," said Gwyn.

It was a joke between us. When Gwyn had moved back to Las Abs last year, she had seen me and remembered about my mom's death and felt sorry for me.

"There you were at the track, pretty much *daring* anyone to come over, looking like the opposite of someone I would have said hi to in Orange County. And me, thinking, oh, what the hell. I'm going to go rattle that girl's cage. And bestow my everlasting friendship upon her."

I snorted.

"So be nice to me or I am dumping you like last year's high heels."

"Slow down—cops like to hang out here." I pointed to the speed limit sign as it flashed by.

"So what did you do with yourself before I came along?" asked Gwyn.

"I ran a lot."

"Yeah, but, you can't run all day."

I laughed. "Can, too!"

"Wow. So you ran for eight years straight? 'Til I said hi?" she asked.

"Let's just say I know these roads really, really well."

"Ma would *kill* me if I ran the roads around here. You got some kind of death-wish?"

I looked down.

"Oh, Sam," she said, flushing deep red. "I'm sorry."

"No, it's okay. You don't have to do that . . . that walking-on-eggshells thing with me."

"O-kaaaay," she said.

"I mean it. Truly. I like that you speak your mind."

"Yeah," she said. "Before my brain has a chance to catch up."

"Exactly." I'd wished for years that someone would simply *talk* to me instead of looking all sorry for me. "At least you say words."

"Hey, Sam?" She bit her lip. "No eggshells, right?"

"Just say it."

"Ma said there was a girl with your mom and she died, too."

"Maggie. She was my best friend. She was driving with me and Mom that evening. Maggie had her new kitten with her and she let me hold it. She made a big deal about how I had to hold on no matter what, but when we stopped at my house, the kitten clawed me and I let go. It jumped out the car door and ran into the street, and that's why Maggie and Mom were in the road when the drunk driver struck them down. This is another speed-trap," I said, pointing to an upcoming twenty-five mile-per-hour sign. "Sorry." I sighed. "I'm a little hyper-aware when it comes to cars and driving."

"I would be, too."

We pulled into the SIERRA CARES Animal Advocates parking lot, and Gwyn picked up three rescue kittens. As we climbed back into the car, she said it felt awful not taking more.

"Like it's my fault the rest of them could die," she

said.

"Sierra Cares is a no-kill facility," I pointed out. "Besides, you can't rescue every cat in the state of California. You shouldn't feel guilty."

"Well, I *do*, and I don't care how I'm *supposed* to feel."

I knew all about having to conform to what you're supposed to feel. I'd learned early on to tell counselors that I knew Mom's and Maggie's deaths weren't my fault rather than confess how I really felt.

I was quiet on the drive back, thinking of Mom, worrying about Will, but Gwyn talked enough for both of us.

"So what do you think?" she asked. I realized I had no idea what she'd been talking about.

"I'm sorry," I said. "I spaced out—what did you ask me?"

"Rufus. What do you think about adoption?"

Rufus. Fluffy grey cat who apparently didn't spend much time in the kitty-apartments. "Um, you mean me? Adopt Rufus?"

"Hello. Yes. You."

I stared awkwardly at my feet.

"Oh. My. God. I'm such an idiot. You probably can't stand cats after . . ." She squeezed my hand as we pulled into my driveway. Leaning over, she gave me a huge hug. "Forget about the cat. And forget everything I said about Will and his sister. I'm sure he's a very nice person with no dark secrets to hide."

I smiled and said goodbye.

Gwyn drove off and my phone buzzed. It was Will. Asking if he could come pick me up for dinner because his sister wanted to talk.

Now.

8

LETTER FROM FRANCE

"Is he allowed to drive teens without his sister?" asked my dad. Which meant that at least one person in Las Abs didn't know Will and I had come back alone last night.

Sylvia murmured that it was only a mile.

"Does your license allow you to drive someone my age?" I asked Will over the phone.

Will laughed on the other end. "I'm eighteen, remember?"

"Right," I replied.

I told Syl and my dad what Will said, and my dad nodded his "Okay."

"Perfect," Will said. "Give me twenty minutes and I'll be there."

I started to ask why a one-minute drive would take

twenty, but then realized they might want the time to tidy or something.

Will arrived shortly in his sister's Jeep. "What did I tell you about my sister? She started out driving to Fresno this morning, but curiosity changed her mind. She couldn't stand the thought of leaving town now she knows you've got Rippler's Syndrome. She's a pain, but she is so predictable."

"I'm sure she's not as big of a pain as my dad," I said, still embarrassed at having to ask Will before Dad let him drive me one mile.

Will smiled.

"What, no comment about Mr. Safety-Patrol?" I asked.

"There's this thing Mick says: if you can't say anything nice, stow it your seat-back pocket for take-off and landing."

I laughed. "I thought you said she wasn't funny."

"No, I said she doesn't have a sense of humor. She's plenty funny." Will shook his head. "Hey, I've been thinking—how about you train with me? I have some ideas you could try so you'd be more in control of your rippling."

"Training? Absolutely!"

"Okay, then. We'll set something up," Will said.

"Are you going to tell me what this visit's all about?" I asked.

"My sister wants to be the one," Will said. "Tell

you this much though; she's decided to trust you. And she doesn't go halve-sies. When you're in her confidence, you're in all the way."

Outside, heat blasted off the cracked pavement in waves, and I watched a constantly receding mirage, the only hint of water in a parched August. The weeds on either side of our quiet highway had been brown for months; soon the poison oak would flame red across the hills—our fall color.

We arrived at the small cabin and I smelled chocolate.

Mickie greeted me and then turned to her brother. "The timer went off five minutes ago and I took them out."

Brownies. "I hope you didn't go to all this trouble just for me," I said.

"I didn't," Mickie replied. "Will's the chef around here."

Will checked the brownies. "They could have used another couple minutes."

"I did what you said—I took them out when the timer went off."

"I said to test them with a knife first."

"You said to take them out—"

"And *test* them with a knife," Will interrupted.

"Next time, take your own stupid brownies out of the oven."

"Next time I won't make any."

I intervened. "I love gooey brownies. Sylvia always overcooks them because she likes the edges crunchy. Which I think is gross."

"That *is* gross," said Mick and Will in perfect synchronization.

Mickie cleared her throat. "So, as you can see, we are staying put it Las Abuelitas for now."

Will settled at the counter, grinning and cutting vegetables.

"And Will and I have agreed, no more secrets," Mickie said. "Between the three of us."

"How hot do you like your salsa?" Will asked.

"Um, pretty hot is good by me," I replied.

"Will told me you think you rippled for the first time right after your mom's death?" asked Mickie.

She wasn't wasting any time gathering information from me. "That's the first time as far as I know," I said.

"Did you find water calming prior to your mom passing?" she asked.

"Sure," I replied. "I've always liked water. My earliest memories are of times I was staring at the water in the creek or the ocean."

"And you're sure you never rippled any of those times?"

"I am sure I didn't on at least one occasion, because Mom got it on film. If you vanish, you wouldn't show up on film, would you?"

"No," replied Will, laughing. "Of course not."

I shrugged. "It's not like I have a user's manual here."

Mickie frowned at her brother and asked me to tell her about my memory.

"It was the weekend before Mom died, actually. We went to Lake Havasu for a growers' convention. I played on the shore all weekend. Mom forgot my Donald Duck towel and I said the hotel towels were scratchy, and after I complained enough, she let me bring the sheet off my bed instead.

"I remember how the sheet sounded, flapping in the wind. I liked the snapping and fluttering, and I liked how the water looked, and I stood ankle-deep in the lake for ninety-five minutes, mesmerized.

"Mom made a movie of me standing there with the sheet billowing out like a super-hero cape. She forgot to turn it off and that's why I know how long I stood there. Mom set the camera down, thinking it was off, and from then on you see my feet moving in and out of the water."

I lowered my voice. "I still dream about that day at Havasu. I thought of it as the best day of my life for like, forever."

"It certainly sounds like your serotonin levels were elevated," said Mickie. "I wonder why you didn't ripple?"

I tried to remember the last time I'd dreamed of the sheet snapping in the wind and my mother's laughter behind me. It had been awhile. My life was happier now; I needed the dream less and less.

Mickie seemed to notice my shift in mood. "Sorry if that was a hard thing to recall, Sam. I forget to be sensitive sometimes."

Will snorted from the kitchen.

Mickie ignored him. "We have plenty of other things to go over. There's some information we'd like to share with you."

Will hummed as he chopped through a bunch of cilantro. "Sam, would you juice these limes for me?" He stopped chopping. "Sorry. Go ahead Mick."

He saw my eyes zip to Mickie.

"Mick and me in the kitchen together: *not* good," said Will.

I stepped over to help. The limes scented the hot, stuffy cabin with citrus.

"You going to show her the letter before we're senior citizens?" asked Will.

Mickie made a sound that combined growling and grunting and walked to a desk. Will laughed noiselessly.

"Step over here when *Chef Will* decides to release you," Mickie said.

She stood at a small, crowded table that functioned as a desk. Their home was compact; kitchen and family room occupied one room together. On the wall beside the desk I saw a map of the world. There were red dots concentrated in various countries, the heaviest concentration of dots in locations that I knew recreated a map I'd looked at before. There were lots of dots immediately north of where Las Abuelitas snuggled into the base of the Sierra. More dots in the south of France. More in Russia, Alaska, below the Nile River in Egypt. I tried to remember the connection these locations had to one another.

Mick interrupted my reverie. "This July, I began a correspondence with someone claiming to be a friend and colleague of my former advisor, Dr. Pfeffer."

Will chimed in. "Correspondence isn't quite the right word, Mick."

His sister rolled her eyes. "He began sending me information, both written and stuff on encrypted mini-drives. I'm not allowed to write him back—"

"Not that you would have, anyway," Will interrupted.

"I only correspond with coded 'yes' or 'no' answers or simple bits of information that he has me send via personal ads in various small local French newspapers."

"Never thought I'd be using my French to write love letters for my big sister," Will said.

"Will, stuff it, already!" snapped his sister.

"Especially to some ninety year old dude."

Mickie closed her eyes and moved her lips like she was counting to ten.

She continued. "So here's what we know so far. The letter-writer, Waldhart de Rochefort—"

"I call him Sir Walter," said Will. "You'll see why when you get a look at his handwriting."

"—whom Will calls Sir Walter, used to spy on Dr. Helmann in his lab in Nazi Germany. Apparently he was very worried about what Helmann was up to at that time. And he thinks that the current threat to carriers of Helmann's disease began at that time."

"What makes you think you can trust this Walter-guy?" I asked.

"Easy," said Will. "If he wanted us dead, we'd be history already. He's got a lot of resources at his disposal."

"He's probably too old to come to California and kill us himself," Mickie said. "But he could afford to hire someone to do it."

"Took me awhile to convince Mick on that one, though," said Will.

Suddenly I felt paranoid about this Sir Walter. "What if he plans to kill you later, you know, like get a bunch of information from you first, then kill you?"

"I worried about that," Mickie said. "But I'm reassured on two points. First, he point-blank refuses to let me send him any information, saying that it could be dangerous. Second, he knows all kinds of things that Pfeffer alone could have told him."

Will added, "Like sending letters in wedding invitations, that's something Pfeffer used to do because a wedding invitation can be stuffed full and doesn't look interesting to someone watching your mail. And the password, Twin Rivers."

"Where's Twin Rivers?" I asked.

"Not *where*, but *what*," Mick replied. "It refers to the two rivers after which Will and I were named. Pfeffer and I used to include it in all correspondence, in some innocuous way, as proof of identity and safety."

"So Pfeffer's not dead?" I asked.

"He's dead," she said, sighing. "But Sir Walter is someone he trusted."

That sounded reassuring. I looked at the map again. "Hey, can I ask, what's with the red dots on this map? Is that something to do with my gene?"

"It's a map Pfeffer sent me with a bunch of other stuff right before he was killed," Mickie said. "I don't know what it marks. I'm dying to ask Sir Walter if he knows, but that would be breaking his rules on our correspondence."

"Sir Walter sent us an identical map," Will said. "Part of his proof that he was friends with Pfeffer."

"Sir Walter wrote as though he thought I'd know what the map meant already," said Mickie. "The map he sent was printed on Pfeffer's crappy Big Bertha printer. You can see where it skips in all the same places."

"These locations remind me of something," I said.

"The meteorites with that element, toviasite. No, no—tobiasite," Will said. "From the Geology unit last year."

Geology. *Right!* That was where I'd seen a map marked up like this. I'd actually *made* a map highlighting these locations. "Not meteorites, Will—gold. These are all places where significant gold mining has taken place."

Will walked toward us. "I did a report on those meteorites. The red dots mark places they were found." He extended an avocado-smeared finger towards the map.

"Respect the research, man!" Mickie slapped Will's messy hand away. "Don't you have things to finish up in the kitchen?"

Will shrugged and walked back, licking his fingers clean like a cat. I swallowed and looked away from him, concentrating on *not* thinking about his mouth, his lips.

"I did a report on gold mining. For the same class. And I'm sure about these locations," I said.

"Maybe." Will didn't sound convinced. "I still say it's meteorites. Except they missed Las Abs."

"We have meteorites?" I asked.

"We had one. That's why I did the report. It was found over by Bella Fria. In the hot springs."

"So why isn't Las Abuelitas lit up on this map?" I asked. "We have both: gold and the meteor."

"Are you for sure about the gold mining, Sam?" asked Mickie. "Will showed me his tobiasite meteor map. It matched up pretty well."

I flushed. "I'm sure. I didn't save my map, but you

can google it."

"No, I believe you," Mickie said.

"So this messes with my theory that people with Helmann's are like magnets for meteorites," Will said.

"That's not a theory, Will. That's a load of crap. You think astrophysicists would have failed to notice if meteors started veering off their trajectories in order to hit certain people?"

Will smiled, shrugged. "I have a theory. You got nada, Mick."

Mickie rolled her eyes and muttered something unintelligible except for the words *idiot* and *theory*. "Is dinner done?"

"Two minutes," said Will.

"And the maps are identical?" I asked.

"Nearly," said Mickie. "I'll grab the other one." She crossed to the hall and kicked her bedroom door open.

The maps looked the same. Except for coffee stains, I couldn't find any differences at first. Then I noticed a list of locations penned in at the bottom of both maps, numerous towns listed under the heading of California, U.S.A. All gold-rush towns, listed in alphabetical order. At the bottom, "Bella Fria" had been added in pencil.

I pointed to "Bella Fria." "That's the abandoned mining town right by us."

"Yeah," said Mickie. A phantom smile flickered briefly across her face. "Pfeffer said we'd be safe here in his final letter."

"He rented us this house," said Will. "He didn't say anything about how safe we'd be here."

"What else does 'Bella Fria looks promising' mean, coming from a man who knew he was about to be killed, pea-brain?" asked his sister.

Will shrugged in response, then added, "Dinner's ready."

I sat down in front of the coffee table that doubled as their dining table. "Smells awesome," I said.

Will grinned. "Hey, Mick, you want to get your nose out of the map? We're eating here."

"I'm checking something," said Mickie.

"When Mick was, uh, driving back from Fresno earlier today, she picked up tamales and fresh corn tortillas from my favorite taco truck. To make peace. And to force me to make my *pico de gallo*." Will flashed a huge white grin as he set the salsa down.

My heart and stomach flopped around like fish out of water as two different hungers competed inside me. I turned my attention to the food. The salsa pretty much lit my mouth on fire, and I grabbed extra sour cream to cool the burn.

"Sir Walter's map doesn't have 'Bella Fria' hand-written on it, whatever that means," said Mickie. She grabbed a plate and joined us, taking a quick bite before continuing. "So gold and tobiasite aside, it looks like Sir Walter was someone Pfeffer trusted enough to send a map to," Mick said. She grabbed the sour cream from my side of the coffee table. "Spicy, much, Will?"

He grinned. "It's good, huh?"

Mick passed a letter to me. The handwriting looked like it was written with a feather pen, all tidy with elegant curlicues. "The first letter he sent us."

I began to read.

My dear Ms. Mackenzie Baker,

I wish to present myself to your notice as a colleague, and a friend, of the late Professeur Pfeffer. He spoke to me of you in terms of highest praise, both for your intelligence and the remarkable caution with which you have thus far preserved the safety of your interesting sibling. As someone with more than a bit of "interesting" myself, I am able to sympathize with the difficulties this must present to you.

I should like to suggest a correspondence between us, as I believe that I have the ability and knowledge to be of usefulness to yourself and your brother, whose name Dr. Pfeffer has withheld from me. Also, I confess I wonder if you might be of usefulness to myself. But more of this at a future time.

I enclose a copy of a map sent to me by my dear friend before his demise. Perhaps you will recognize it. It marks sites which are of mutual interest to all of us who esteemed Pfeffer's work.

If you should choose that our correspondence continues, perhaps you would be so kind as to notify me by means of the enclosed form.

Believe me to be,

Your sincerest well-wisher,
Waldhart de Rochefort

Will turned to me, "You're going on that trip to France, right? Maybe you can meet him."

"I'm not involving Sam in our problems." Mickie glared at her brother.

"He wants to meet with us," Will said. "But Mick has this thing about accepting charity, and no way can we afford a trip to Europe."

"Shut up," said his sister.

"The French Club group needs another chaperone," I said. "Chaperones travel free, but it's not charity. It's hard work, according to Sylvia. She went with her niece's class before she and my dad got together, and she won't do it again for anything."

"I don't have a problem with Sir Walter paying my way," said Will. "But you go ahead and earn your way."

"Hmmph," grunted Mickie.

It was obvious she wanted to change the subject.

"So, de Rochefort, er, Sir Walter, was alive during World War Two?" I asked.

"Give her the second letter," said Mickie, nodding.

"Here's the important part," Will said, pointing to the second page.

I have a long acquaintance with Monsieur Docteur Helmann and his investigations into the many secrets about the irregularity that bears his name. As you have probably guessed, I have good means to secure myself against being discovered. I did what I could, during the Second World War, to lessen some of the atrocities he committed or contemplated. After the war, he disappeared, residing, I believe, in your own country of America. I guessed this because the manufacturing of Neuroprine, one of the chemicals he used for his human experimentations, began in your country shortly after his disappearance.

Well, I thought, perhaps he has turned to philanthropy after all. Or succumbed to his desire for riches, the least distasteful of his appetites. Whatever his original intention, he has embarked upon a dark path once more. You will be aware of the deaths of Professors Ryan, Garrett, Jacobsen, and Pfeffer. With these and other deaths, I have, alas, lost contact with anyone in your country who might provide insight into Helmann's plans or deeds. But he must be stopped. This is clear to me at last, as it will be to you when you have viewed the enclosed.

I looked up, trying to remember the dates for World War Two. "So he's what: seventy, eighty years old?"

"We think he's eighty-eight or older, guessing he was at least fourteen the first year I know Helmann to have been involved in researching Helmann's Disease," Mickie said.

"Given that he's chosen to write us letters instead of visit, we're guessing he doesn't have the stamina for a long trip," Will said.

"So, is it just me, or do you both think he's dropping hints all over that he ripples?" I asked.

"Hard to be certain," Mickie replied.

"Oh, I think that's what he's talking about. What else could he mean?" Will asked.

"Well," Mickie began, her voice dripping sarcasm. "We could make any number of guesses as to what he means and be wrong a hundred times."

"He's a rippler," Will muttered.

"Here." Mickie handed me a French newspaper clipping. "He sent this along with letter two."

"Le Monde?" I asked. "This is the big Paris paper. Like the Wall Street Journal except for France."

I began reading and translating an article printed two weeks ago about Helmann's Disease.

"It says a total of two-hundred sixty-three Helmann's carriers responded to an email offer for a reduced cost Neuroprine-substitute and they're all dead now," Will said.

"That's crazy," I whispered.

"Yeah." Mickie's expression was cold and hard. "I'm guessing this was what kept him busy the past few weeks."

"You have to meet him, Mickie," I said. "You have to tell him everything you know. This is terrible."

"What do you want to bet the same person behind the deaths here in the United States was behind those murders?" Will asked.

"I need to find out what the red dots mean." Mickie sighed. "I need to speak with Waldhart de Rochefort."

Excerpted from the private journal of Girard L'Inferne, approx. 1400

I saw her leave today and followed. She left alone. But to meet him; they arrived by design, I am certain. Beside the river, where the willows grow to the water's edge, I saw them. Side by side they lay; gazing into one another's eyes they whispered. Sometimes Waldhart would make to press his lips upon hers, but ever, when he tried, she became air, shivering away from his touch, I thought.

This is good, I let myself say. She likes him not.

Closer I edged, to hear what they spoke. It was nothing to give my heart pleasure.

"Lisaba, you know I will marry you regardless," spoke he.

She drew her dark brows together. "I know."

"Nor will I seek another lover. I can live as the brothers at the monastery so long as I have you beside me," said he.

She sighed, running her hand upon his face and withdrawing it quickly as though burned. "I can have no child if I marry you."

"That is your reason?" he asked.

"Yes. And if I produce no heir Louis receives our lands and all they contain. These things you know already."

He grunted, leaned to kiss her. She faded to air and returned to her flesh.

She continued. "If we wed there would be no child unless I lay with another man. Is that what you are asking of me?"

He turned from her, an angry look I knew well played across his face. "Come away with me," he whispered.

"Never," she said.

Both lay silent a long while.

At last I saw a tear and then another upon his cheek. The weakling.

She turned to him, wiping his face as I have seen her do for a brat who has spilled himself upon the Great Hall floor. But then she kissed him, and as he turned his body to her, she vanished. He groaned. She reappeared. This same manner of thing happened twice again.

My anger burned as though it would consume the forest, but I could not look away. Again, they embraced, always she faded but then returned.

"It is no use, heart of mine," she said to him at last, pulling back from his kiss.

And I knew.

I knew.

Her heart would never be mine. Though she wed me, though he should perish in battle, though all the world should change. She would love him still.

I felt the presence of the great boar before I saw him. A fearsome tusked thing. Come here, I called. Come here.

Lo, it approached. Snuffling, pawing, unheard by the lovers at the brook.

Gouge them, crush them, spill their blood, said I to the great beast. The creature looked about him, lowered his potent head, and trotted forth to ruin my enemies.

Who has done what I have done? Who is like me, that he can control the beasts of the forest? Alas, I did not bid the boar to *be silent. He squealed a hideous sound which gave the pair time to disappear into air, mightily puzzling the creature.*

I have lost, thought I.

But no. This day has seen me victorious.

This evening, Helisabat de Rochefort pledged herself to be mine.

-translation by G. Pfeffer

9

HITTING THE WALL

"Sounds like one of us skipped breakfast," Will said as my stomach growled noisily on our way to school the next day.

I'd slept in late and skipped eating a real breakfast in order to bike to school with Will. Syl made me take a couple of cereal bars. I pulled one out, tore the wrapper with my teeth and pushed my breakfast up from the bottom of the plastic wrapper, remembering another of my questions about rippling.

"How long does it take to get hungry or thirsty when you're invisible?"

Will's brows contracted as he thought about it. "I went once for three days without food or water."

"Seriously?"

"Two summers ago, Mickie had to leave for job

training for four days. It wouldn't have been a big deal except she forgot to leave me grocery money. So I ate my way through all the bread and cereal in the house the first morning and afternoon. For dinner it was peanut butter on an apple half, peanut butter on zucchini, and peanut butter on red bell peppers. That was nasty; take my word for it.

"So I ripple for the next three days 'til Mick gets back so that I won't feel hungry. Then she comes back in the house and she's all looking in the fridge, shouting at me about why didn't I leave her some food 'cause she's starving after four days of cafeteria food," he said, laughing. "It was pretty funny seeing her face when I told her *why* there wasn't any food in the apartment."

"You should have grabbed food from next door, you know, a little something from everyone, not like a huge raid on any one person. I mean, you could walk through walls."

He frowned. "Nah, that's too much like something my dad would do. I take a pop-tart from someone, it's stealing."

I nodded, but I was pretty sure I'd have stolen the stupid pop-tart. My life was sheltered, easy. I'd never seen our fridge or pantry empty. Anytime I wanted something, I only had to mention it to Sylvia. I had never imagined things any different.

"Hey, Sam," Will interrupted my ruminations, "you still want to walk through walls?"

My face lit up. "Heck, yeah!"

"I was thinking that could be a fun way to kick off our training, you know, like we talked about. Assuming we're still on . . ."

"We're totally on." I needed practice, control.

We made plans for Will to give me a tour of Las Abs where he would show me some of his favorite things to walk through. He felt that with my being newer at the whole thing it would be safer to do this at night. He also gave me homework, insisting that I practice rippling and reappearing on my own for a few days.

"Great," I said. "Because it's not like I'm going to get any homework today or anything."

"We don't want to repeat having you materialize inside anything. I want you to ripple away and practice telling yourself to look and make sure you're clear first before you ripple solid," he said.

I continued through the first day of school, gathering homework. At lunch, Will and I sat together, and today Gwyn joined us. She fluttered from clique to clique in our small high school, like she didn't acknowledge the well-defined barriers the rest of us saw. And everyone just let it happen, because everyone liked Gwyn.

She sat and launched into the woes of being the daughter of Bridget Li. "Ma's forcing me to take AP Biology," she whined. "Which means I'm already behind. Did you guys know about the research project over the summer?"

Will nodded and I said, "Yes."

"I don't know what I'm going to do," she said, laying her head down on the table in mock despair.

"Buy a really good paper online?" I suggested.

"Sam!" Gwyn raised her head and glared at me.

"Just kidding," I said.

"You can join Sam and me, on our project," said Will.

Gwyn beamed at him. "I knew there was a reason I sat down here," she said, unwrapping her sandwich. "Great. Organic PB-n-J on whole grain bread. Again." She stared longingly at my preservative-laden ham and swiss on sourdough.

"Just take it." I passed her my sandwich.

All that week I practiced, getting ready for our Sunday night rippling "class." Control meant secrecy. Secrecy meant safety from whoever wanted me dead. It didn't hurt that I expected to have some fun learning this control.

My dad was down in the Valley with one of the berry farms. Sylvia gave me an 11:30 PM curfew, more than generous seeing as I was crashed out most nights by 9:45.

Will came by for me as the sun was setting.

"There're all kinds of places for brick walls; there's

Bridget and Gwyn's for a rock wall—did you know they live in the town's oldest building?" asked Will.

I nodded as he continued.

"And the school cafeteria has those big glass windows that are almost like walls. I think you'll like glass a lot. Then we could try the gym for cinder-block; I don't know if you'll *like* it, but it's interesting."

I realized how nervous I felt now that we were actually going to do this. I mean, we were talking about walking through *solid objects* here. I thought we could avoid a disaster like at the creek, but it was still a sobering reminder that Will didn't know everything.

He glanced over at me as we pulled into the Murietta Park parking lot. "You okay, Sam? You're so quiet."

"I'm scared."

"I thought ahead. Check this out." He pulled out the small camera he'd taken on our trip to Yosemite.

My heart fell to the bottom of my stomach. "You're going to film this?"

"No, I have some footage of Illilouette Creek to calm you. Water, right?"

"You're a genius."

He shrugged. "You know the willows here in the park? Well, they're not exactly a wall, but the branches form a solid mass, and you like running your hand through them, so I'm thinking maybe we could start there?"

I smiled. "Perfect."

We walked across the parking lot to the willow cluster. Will turned on the camera. It was dark now: the screen threw off light like a flashlight.

"I'm setting this to loop continuously," he explained, pushing buttons.

"Would you mind going first, just so . . . I don't know; I think it would be easier if I watched you first."

"Sure." Will smiled and turned to the trees.

A breath of wind passed us, and the willows rustled in response, a whispering chorus. Will approached the murmuring branches, faded and was gone.

He reappeared seconds later with a huge smile. "You're going to love it."

"Yeah, okay." I held out the camera where I could see it.

"The camera is going to go invisible at the same time you do because you're touching it. Just a heads-up."

I nodded. That would have distracted me.

"Oh, and Sam, one more thing."

"Yeah?"

"Step away from the branches before you come back. In case branches explode like water."

I nodded, trying to smile. I looked at the tiny bright screen and saw the creek in miniature perfection. The water looked glassy-still, but as I watched, a pine needle cluster worked free from a rock and spun lazily into the current and out of the frame. The image rippled away. My invisible lips smiled, confidence coursing through me. I turned to the willows.

Leaves and branches tickled their way right through me. I wanted to giggle. I caught a scent component: greenish, damp, and full of life. Maybe it was even a flavor rather than a scent. I turned to take another pass—again, the fresh soothing taste passed through my mind. Again, the willows shivered against me as I moved ghostly-smooth in my invisible state.

Incredible. I had to tell Will about it. I rippled solid.

"It's like I have to invent words for what that felt like, and the incredible taste—wow!"

We tried out different words for the sensation of the willow branches as they passed through us: "prickly" and "needling" we rejected, "slithery" and "ticklish" worked.

"You'll like passing through glass if you liked that," he said. "But it's too early to risk being seen in front of school. We should probably wait 'til after midnight for that."

"My curfew's 11:30."

"Oh. Right. So maybe we head over to the bakery now? You've got to try a rock wall." He grinned eagerly at me.

I nodded and we turned to walk down Main Street. "How did you figure out you could walk through walls? That must have taken some nerve the first time."

"My dad threw me at our fireplace when I was seven. Instinct kicked in and the next thing I knew I was invisible and sailing right through this screechy brick wall. I stood outside, trying to figure out what happened, and if I was dead or alive. A few days later, I got curious enough to try walking through."

"Um, did you just say your dad *threw* you at a brick wall?"

"Yeah. He was pretty drunk."

"You could have died. What was he thinking?"

He shrugged as we walked on. "He storms in one night shouting for money. I ripple and hide behind the couch 'cause I'm scared. He grabs Mickie and puts her in a headlock and calls for Mom, saying how he's gonna squeeze Mick's brains out if Mom doesn't bring him some money right *now*.

"I'm watching all this from behind the couch and Mom comes out of the kitchen and sees Mickie and freezes, tells him to let go of her, she's a child, stuff like that. Dad's shouting even louder how he knows she's hiding a hundred thousand dollars somewhere in the house, and she better get it quick. She grabs an envelope she got at the bank that afternoon. I'd been with her and watched them count it out, and I know it's only a couple hundred, so I'm getting pretty scared what he'll do if he counts it. Plus Mickie's face is a bad color, and I'm thinking he might actually kill her this time."

Will paused to point me into the alley beside

Bridget and Gwyn's.

He continued. "Then after Mom gives him the money, he clocks her and she goes down like a rag doll. I just lose it. I mean, I actually see *red* for a couple seconds. I ripple solid and charge him. I get a couple of good soccer kicks in on his shins before he even notices me. But when he sees it's *me* hurting his shins, he drops Mickie like she's on fire and grabs me. He doesn't even take any swipes, just throws me at the fireplace."

I realized I'd been holding my breath and let it out.

"You okay?" he asked.

"Me? Sure, I'm fine. I didn't have to *live* that. Geez, Will. And how'd you turn out like, one of the nicest people I've ever met when you had all *that* to deal with?"

Will shrugged. "Growing up with my dad around, I knew exactly what I *didn't* want to be. With Mom, we always knew what it meant to be loved. Maybe it would have been different without her. I wish you could have met her."

"Me, too."

It felt like peeling through an onion-skin layer of honesty.

Will punched me on the shoulder. "Nicest person you ever met. Give me a friggin' break."

The rawness of the moment passed.

"You up for some breaking and entering, without the breaking?" asked Will.

I smiled, letting the weight of his story slide off my shoulders.

Will said he could go first, and I nodded. I still needed proof that this was possible. *Of course you won't actually see him do it—he'll be invisible*, a part of me said. But even as I heard that small voice, I realized that the truth was I trusted Will, completely.

"Here goes nothing." He winked at me as he rippled.

A minute later he rematerialized, beaming like a kid with a new bike.

"Rock walls are so sick! Wish our house was made of rock. Okay, you go now." He reached down to switch the camera to the creek video again.

I held the camera in front of me. I was calmer and this time I rippled right away.

Walking through a wall didn't sound like a strange idea anymore. I felt invincible. The feeling seemed to accompany rippling. Without fear, I passed into the wall of Bridget's bakery kitchen.

The flavor was sand. Or what a river-beach would smell like on a warm day. Dry, a bit of desert-dustiness to it. The physical echoes were harder for me to place. I ran my hand back through the wall again and decided that if I were an hour-glass with sand running through me, this might be how I'd feel. It was unmistakably pleasant—Will had that right—almost like something I'd felt some other time, but I couldn't place when or where. Then I laughed. It was almost exactly like the feeling of sand as I poured buckets over my hands when I was little.

I passed back through the wall, a delicious whisper of sand, and saw kids loitering at the mouth of the alley. I wanted to tell Will how right he was about rock walls. As I waited for the kids to leave, I moved closer to Will, leaning against him, which I figured would freeze him in an obvious way and let him know I'd passed back into the alley.

He grunted a small laugh. He knew I was here. We waited for the loiterers to leave. I moved away from Will and spun on one foot, flinging my arms out like an ice-skater. The lack of resistance against whatever "me" existed felt so cool. If I were visible, I'd be doing perfect spirals. I continued spinning, never dizzy, but very aware of the sense that my arms and even my ponytail were flung out from me in some "real" sense. I scooted closer to the wall so I could pass through the falling-beach-sand sensation while spinning

He called to me, a stage whisper, "Sam—they left."

I prepared to ripple back solid beside the corner of the building, spinning one last time and noting the same sensations that my invisible body had reality, from toes to pulled-back hair.

Just as I came solid, a shotgun report blasted out, so near it deafened me. A rain of fine gravel and small rocks followed the sound.

I yelled in pain as a rock caught my jaw and another clipped my shoulder.

Will grabbed for me, trying to pull me away from the shower of debris. "Your hair," he said. He pointed to a small hole blasted through the wall of Bridget's kitchen, right beside the corner. Several cats were growling behind us—a low, eerie noise.

I didn't see the connection between the wall and my hair. And then I did see it. "My ponytail did that?" I asked, pointing to the hole.

"It was 'in' the rock wall as you materialized," he said. "Your hair displaced the wall."

I cringed, imagining what could have happened if it had been my arm or leg.

We heard shouting. Perhaps ten seconds had passed after the explosion. "Over there: the alley," shouted a deep, male voice.

Within seconds, a police car siren wound to life.

"Let's ripple. Now," said Will, vanishing.

I tried to still my heart. "I don't think I can," I said to thin air.

Will reappeared, looking around for additional ways to escape.

There were none.

10

ROCK STAR

We were blocked in, buildings on either side of us, an eight-foot fence running the width of the dead-end alley before becoming the back-side of the cat kennels. Cats yowled, making freaky noises I didn't think should come out of a cat. The police car approached, lights bouncing into the alley.

"I'll hide in the cat kennels," I said. "You ripple!"

I dashed to the closest one, lifted the latch, and let myself in. I saw Will hesitate. What was he doing? I watched through the tiny cat kennel windows, one on each corner. Will took a running leap at the fence, grabbed the top, and hauled himself up, lit by oncoming headlights. The patrol car paused for a moment as Will disappeared over the fence. Then the vehicle backed out of the alley rapidly, tires squealing as it raced down Main to catch him on the other side.

"Dear God, let him have the sense to ripple this time," I whispered as I backed away from the window. A cat hissed and another clawed the back of my left leg. I kept silent, lips pulled thin and tight from the sudden, sharp pain. I had no light now that the police car had backed away. That had been Will's goal, of course. He'd stayed visible to lead the cops away from me. The stupid idiot.

A look out the window revealed a handful of onlookers milling in the alley, pointing to the hole in the wall. I drew back into the shadows, amidst anxious felines. I heard a door open, the back entrance to Gwyn's home. Gwyn and her mom were arguing.

"You called the police, Ma, let them do their job." That was Gwyn's voice.

"Las Abs' finest aren't going to take care of my kids." Bridget's voice, referring to her feline "children." "Run grab me the kitty Xanax. Woody Allen is going to need one."

What if "Woody Allen" was in this kennel? So. Not. Good.

Gwyn unlocked a storage door under the stairwell. She fumbled inside and called out, "How many?"

"He doesn't look good. Bring me two."

"Where are you?" Gwyn again.

"I'm in apartment one. Honestly, Gwyn, it's not

like I move the cats around."

I must be in "five," since this was the fifth from the left.

"Gwyn, check on everyone in number two, will you? See how Jet Li's doing."

But Gwyn apparently had her own ideas. I heard her storming towards me and I froze.

"Do you mind?" She sounded ticked. "The cats are totally freaked, and having all of you making noise out here isn't helping."

She was speaking to the group in the alley.

"Here, someone dropped this camera," said one voice as the others receded.

Will's camera! And me the opposite of chillaxed. I thought with envy of Will's easy control of his talent.

And I had an idea.

"Don't over-exert yourself, Gwyn." Bridget's voice dripped sarcasm. "I'll take a look at Jet Li."

"Chill, Ma. I was kicking everyone out of the alley."

I tried to focus on the pull of Will's arm, strong and comforting as the wall had exploded around me minutes ago.

"Oh." Bridget's voice, repentant. "That was very thoughtful of you."

I recalled the warmth of his touch, remembered the exact spot where his fingers pressed into my skin.

"I'm checking number three," Gwyn said.

I thought how those fingers would feel tracing my

jaw line, my lips.

"Gwyn! Rufus isn't home," said Bridget, opening number four.

I remembered Will's arms pulling me to safety from Illilouette Creek. I could almost feel it.

"You can't let him wander at night." Bridget, a zillion miles away.

"Like I'm the boss of him." Gwyn, muttering.

Warm and safe in Will's arms, I felt myself slip into serene invisibility.

Gwyn opened the door to kennel five, my kennel. I straightened up and passed through the cat house wall as cats renewed their strange guttural moans. The wall was scent-tainted with cats marking their territory. No way was I *ever* passing through these walls again. I'd let the police haul me off in hand-cuffs first.

I glided silently back to the park, quiet as the nocturnal creatures I passed. Twice, dogs followed my progress with bright eyes; one barked. When I reached the car, it was empty and my pulse picked up speed. Where was Will? I rippled solid, tried the door. It opened and I climbed in.

Will rippled solid in the driver's seat, and I let out a squeak.

We backed out of the parking lot. "You've got nine minutes," he said. "Good timing!"

He remembered my curfew.

It hadn't even crossed my mind.

"You look like you're freezing," he said, as we pulled onto Main, creating a breeze in the open-topped Jeep. "Here." He tossed me his hoodie, warm and soft and smelling like Will.

"Someone found your camera," I said. "I must have dropped it when I ran to the cat house. I'm really sorry."

"No big deal."

"Gwyn will look at the pictures. She's going to know it's either yours or Mickie's. You could end up in trouble."

"I'll say I lost it. No worries."

We turned off Main onto the old highway that both our homes sat on.

And suddenly I was giggling. I'd walked through a wall!

"Hey Will—I walked through a freaking rock wall tonight!"

He laughed—a deep, throaty guffaw.

"I'm like, a *rock-star*."

"You did *not* just say that, man."

I giggled again and Will laughed along with me.

I took a deep breath as we picked up speed. I threw my head back, raised my arms and hollered to the ink-black sky, "I'M A ROCK STAR! WAAAAA-HOOOOO!"

I slept great, the opposite of what I'd expected after

a harrowing evening with a boy I was now officially obsessing over. I showered and dressed, taking the stairs two at a time on my way to breakfast. That's when I caught a glimpse of myself in the hall mirror. A large, purplish bruise bloomed to the side of my chin. I pushed on it. Bad idea. I winced.

"Hey, Sylvia, do you have some cover-up I can borrow?" I pointed to the ugly bruise.

"That looks awful," she said. Something in her voice made my dad look up from his paper. "How'd it happen?" She walked to her desk and came back rummaging through her purse.

"I walked into a wall." *And out the other side.*

I took the cover-stick from Sylvia and walked to the mirror hanging over the fireplace at the far end of our combination kitchen and family room. While I applied cover-up, I saw my dad, in the mirror, staring pointedly at Sylvia—non-verbals flying back and forth between them.

"You were out with the Baker kid." Dad said it like an accusation.

"Will," I replied. "From cross country."

My dad's brows pulled together. "Did he hit you?"

I stared in shock.

Sylvia whispered, "Dave!"

"Answer me, Samantha. Did he hit you?"

I looked my dad straight in the eyes. "Of course not," I replied, my voice icy.

"He's not that kind of boy," said Sylvia. I silently blessed her for coming to Will's defense.

"I hear his dad was."

"Will's *not* like his dad," I said.

"You're not trying to cover for him, are you Sam?"

"Dad, if I *were* trying to cover for him, do you seriously think I'd come down here and show this to you?" I pointed to the bruise.

Sylvia passed me a bowl of oatmeal, loaded with brown sugar, cream and syllaberries.

"I'm going to my room to eat," I said.

I could hear Sylvia's voice as I thumped up the stairs. "Dave, if anyone knows the signs to look for, it's me. You know that."

I didn't want to hear his response. I slammed the door—my response. But the ducting relayed Sylvia's calm, sensible tones.

"Believe me: Sam coming down here asking for cover-up for that bruise is proof that she's not someone who would hide if there were anything *to* hide."

True enough, I realized. If a boy hit me, I wouldn't keep quiet about it. Of course, I'd also kick the crap out of him, thanks to the self-defense lessons Syl made me take three years ago: *"A woman needs to know how to deliver a good kick to the cojones."*

"I want to keep her safe," Dad said.

"You can't always do that. You have to trust her."

My dad sighed heavily and I began shoveling

133

mouthfuls of oatmeal. Will would be by in less than five minutes.

I heard his knock at 6:40 and I scampered down the stairs to get there first. "I'm leaving," I hollered, slamming the door behind me.

"Morning," Will said. We took off on our bikes. "I've been trying to figure something out. Why on earth would your ponytail stick straight out from your head?"

"My ponytail?"

"Yeah, when you rippled back and your hair displaced all that rock. Your hair was sticking out straight."

"I'd been spinning in circles. Guess I should be still when I ripple solid."

"You think?" he asked laughing. "So how'd you get away, without the camera to help you ripple?"

I flushed, grabbed my water-tube and took a long pull, giving me time to think before answering. I so wasn't going to tell him the truth. If I hinted to Will how I felt, and he didn't feel the same way? Instant awkward. "I used a mental image instead."

"Good thinking." Will's dark eyes caught mine and he lowered his voice. "I really hated leaving you there. But I figured you had my camera. I was debating coming to find you, but I worried we'd cross paths and miss each other. Man, I was glad to see you ripple back!"

I turned back to face the road, but I was smiling.

"Were you scared?" Will asked.

"Terrified! Bridget and Gwyn were going from room to room in the cat kennels. I barely got away."

"So, not only did you ripple using a visual image, you did it scared? Those are good signs of control, Sam."

My smile grew to a grin as we rounded onto Main Street.

"Plus, it shows you think well under pressure."

You have no idea, I thought. "What about you? Were you worried? I mean, the police have a description of you, don't they?"

He laughed. "Adult male, approximately five-foot-nine, a hundred-thirty pounds, wearing jeans and a black hoodie, hood worn up. So they were looking for someone shorter and smaller than me. Plus my hoodie's grey. Anyways, I'd have told the truth. That I heard what sounded like a shot and took off scared."

"Thanks for taking them off my trail."

"No worries. I'm glad it worked. And we still need to go out again, another night, and try the plate glass at the cafeteria. Sometime when you can get clearance for a later curfew."

Yeah. That'll happen. I felt bitter, remembering my dad's suspicions. The track loomed ahead, less than a block away.

"If you want to, I mean. I just think you'd like glass. I guess you could try it on your own, though.

You've got that sliding glass door." His tone was uncertain.

He'd mistaken my silence for reluctance. "No, no," I said. "Together would be much better." I looked over and smiled.

We rode our bikes across the school parking lot towards the track and veered to where Gwyn was stretching.

"Hey, Gwyn," I called.

"Did you guys hear about the major drama last night?" she asked.

I tried to look ignorant, but she wasn't waiting for a response. "Someone fired a shotgun at our building right after 11:00. I figured they were trying to break in and steal the Cat Jar money, but Ma says anyone breaking in would have shot the door lock instead, and that does seem more likely. So maybe someone was shooting at the cats."

Guess she didn't see the *Mythbusters* episode where they prove you can't shoot doors open. But all I said was, "Hmmmm."

"I *know*," she said, as if I'd just agreed with everything. She continued on with a description of the suspect and ended with, "Whoever it was, they stole your camera, Will. I have it at home. Did you know it was missing?" Her eyes were narrowed: was she trying to trip Will up?

"Yeah," Will said, cool and smooth. "I'm glad you

found it."

I bent down to retie my shoe. I wasn't feeling as comfortable as he was.

Gwyn tapped at the back of my leg. "You trying to make friendly with a mean cat?" she asked.

I looked at the scratch marks from last night. "You know me," I said. "Cats just love me."

She studied my face and then changed subjects. "I told Coach I wanted to run with you two, so go easy on me, okay?"

I rolled the enchanting sound of those simple words, "you two," around in my mind as we got through our warm-up laps. Then Coach released us to the 4K.

"You're in charge of the pace," Will said to Gwyn as we took off.

I'd been running with Will for so long that I'd forgotten the rhythm of Gwyn's light tread—five steps for every four that Will and I landed. I vowed to be a better friend to her starting today.

We hit the light on Main Street green and crossed to run past Las ABC. Bridget waved. I could see people evaluating the damage to the rock wall. My stomach clenched. They were going to have to pay for that damage and it was my fault.

"Did you see that old Chinese guy?" Gwyn asked. "Down the alley?"

"Yes," I said, miserable.

Will nodded.

"His great grand-dad built our building. A century and a half ago. Ma's loving his stories." Gwyn's eyes rolled. "She's all about community."

"And cats," Will said.

Gwyn laughed. "Yeah. Hey, that reminds me. Ma says to please beg you to gold-pan, for the fundraiser next weekend."

I'd forgotten all about the event. And now, knowing about my tendency to *vanish* while gazing at peaceful waters, I knew I couldn't consider gold-panning.

My "uh," overlapped with Will's "sure." Was he covering for me? Offering to go so I wouldn't have to? I stared at him, confused.

"It's Labor Day, right?" Will asked.

"Yeah. We have it off, school and cross-country," Gwyn said.

"It sure sounds 'relaxing,'" I said, as a hint to Will in case he'd forgotten that gold-panning occurred in a *creek*.

Will caught my eye, winked. "You can handle a little relaxation, right Sam? I'll be right there to make sure you don't drift off or anything."

"It's not *that* relaxing," said Gwyn. "The water's freezing, for one thing. Honestly, it sounds like hard work."

"What do you say, Sam? You up for some hard

work?" Will asked.

"I guess," I said. I seriously wanted to kick Will.

Half an hour later, we were on our second trip around the 4K, this time minus Gwyn.

"Okay, seriously, what was the 'let's go gold-panning' all about?"

"Sam, we blew a hole in her kitchen wall. It's like the least we can do for Gwyn's mom." He looked at me. "Don't you think?"

"What part of 'me plus water equals ripple' are you not getting?"

"You can do it," he said. "Just keep practicing."

I snorted. "What would your sister recommend?"

Will looked at me, nervous. "Probably better not mention this around her."

We curved by the willows, and I held my arm out, swish-swish-swish, as we ran past.

***

The next few days rushed past in a hot blur. On Thursday, the temperature felt like five-hundred degrees by the last class of the day, and the air conditioner in biology couldn't keep up. I tried to concentrate on a video about DNA strands in humans. Beside me, Gwyn had completely checked out. She slipped me a note.

Come pick up your pledge form for gold panning when we're released from prison. I mean school. You need to catch me up to date on the biology research paper. And I have something to show you. And if you are there Ma might let me take the afternoon off.

I wrote back that I would.

But when Polwen dismissed our class, Will said he needed a minute. I waved Gwyn on ahead.

"What is it?"

"Mick got another wedding invitation in the mail today."

"Did she tell you what it said?"

"Just that it's intriguing."

"I told Gwyn I'd come over."

Will shrugged. "Come by when you're done then, okay?"

I nodded. I *had* to go to Gwyn's first. Not just because she'd asked first. I felt big-time guilty, about what I'd done to the building Gwyn called home. I owed her a lot right now.

I parked my bike in front of Las ABC. The delicious scents were the same; Bridget's smile was the same; but I felt changed. I wanted to disappear as she gave me a quick hug.

"Gwyn said you'd be by." Bridget brushed a stray hair from my face and handed me a pledge form. "Three more day's 'til *Panning for Felines*. We sure appreciate your help."

I smiled back, guilt oozing from every pore of my being.

"You can go through the kitchen; use the door that

leads outside. I gave Gwyn the afternoon off."

I said thanks and stepped out the back to the yard. Against the back fence, Gwyn closed a cat kennel door.

"Hey Sam!" She carried a litter box to the trashcan. "I'm doing a little house-keeping first."

"Your mom said she's giving you the afternoon off."

"This isn't work, according to Ma. Lend me a hand?"

"Can I say no?" I did *not* want to go into those cat-rooms again.

She looked at me, grinning like she thought I was funny. Then her face changed. "Oh. You're not joking."

I hated myself.

"I forgot." She kicked open door number three. "You're not big on cats." She took a moment to reappear during which I agonized over my inability to tell Gwyn the truth.

"Let's go upstairs," she offered as she came back out. "I'll finish later." She soaped her hands at an outdoor sink.

I knew she'd like it better if I protested and offered to help. Would that make up for being a vandal and a liar? I stood by, melting into a warm puddle of guilt.

"I don't mind doing the work now, while it's warm and sunny," Gwyn said. "But I'm not looking forward to cat-care in the winter. I hear you got snow last year."

"Just a little; it looked more like powdered sugar."

"That's more than I want to see. I wish cats hibernated to survive the cold."

"Hibernating *cats*?" I laughed in spite of my solemn mood.

"I'm serious. Wish I could talk Ma into using that Cat Jar money to pay someone to clean the kennels this winter."

"Ask her. There's probably a hundred bucks in there."

"More like six or seven hundred," Gwyn whispered.

"Seriously? She needs to take it to the bank."

"Try telling her that. She'd have to actually close up on time to get to the bank while it's still open."

"Can't you take it in with the daily receipts?" I asked.

Gwyn shook her head. "She wants to ask Mrs. Gutierrez, the bank manager, to match the funds. So, basically, until she stops chatting after closing time, no."

"At the very least, she should take it out of plain view."

"Right." Gwyn laughed. "The whole point is that people see it and donate." She smiled as she finished drying her hands. "Come upstairs. There's something I've been dying to show you. You hungry?"

"Not really. But you grab something, if you want." At the least, I could be agreeable.

"I'm starving." She opened the apartment door at

the top of the enclosed stairwell and bee-lined to the world's smallest refrigerator—the only one in their kitchen—pulling out a plate of leftover pizza. It didn't look like frozen, and I wondered where she'd gotten real pizza.

"Look what I made." She displayed it, proudly.

"You made that?"

"Actually Will made it, but I helped. Turns out he's a very nice guy." She took a huge bite and sighed with pleasure.

"Um, why would Will come here to make pizza?"

"Will heard that Ma doesn't cook dinner—"

"Your mom doesn't cook dinner?"

Gwyn shrugged. "She cooks all day. She's tired by dinner. Anyway, Will says how that's terrible and how he's going to teach me to make pizza so I don't starve to death. He brought it up like five times Tuesday until we finally set a time for him to teach me. He wouldn't let it go, like he was personally responsible for Ma not cooking. Catholic guilt or something." She took another huge bite.

I knew what Will felt guilty for, and it wasn't Bridget's refusal to cook. I *so* should have offered to help with the cats.

I grabbed a slice and took a bite. It was delicious. It looked like plain cheese, but there was nothing ordinary about it.

Gwyn pulled the last slice protectively her direction.

"Hey, I wonder if we could get him to make this for our biology study session Saturday? You need healthy food for your brain to function well."

"Totally," I agreed, taking another bite. "So you ready to get up-to-speed on our research?"

Gwyn groaned. "Hit me."

"It's actually rather interesting," I said. "In a creepy kind of way."

"Creepy?" asked Gwyn, a smile curving her lips. "Like zombies?"

"No, dweeb. Just listen. So we picked 'The History and Future of Eugenics' for our topic."

"Sounds fascinating," said Gwyn. "If I wanted reading material to help me fall asleep. Seriously, Sam, I've never even heard of Eugenics. Can't we pick something interesting like, I don't know, plastic surgery? I could get my boobs done as my contribution."

"Gwyn, please? A little focus here?"

She folded her hands and sat up straight. "I'm all ears."

"Let's say your mom has three milking goats."

"Ma is lactose intolerant."

"Shut up. Let's say one produces three quarts every day, like clockwork. The second produces one quart a day, and the third has chronic infections and produces a pint in a week."

"Shoot the third one," Gwyn muttered.

I ignored her. "Which goat would you breed? The

144

first one, right?"

"I guess," said Gwyn.

"Okay, so imagine my dad working on his syllaberries. If he had two different plants, and let's say one of them yielded three pints of berries a season and one of them yielded one pint, which one would he use for root stock?"

"Duh. The three pint one. Is that seriously how your dad got rich? Eugenics?"

"Eugenics is taking those principles and applying them to humans. But, yeah, I guess that's how dad made it big in farming: Eugenics for plants."

"So, basically, if my mom had dated some guy with man-boobs, I'd be better endowed? That's the kind of thing you're talking about?"

I shook my head. "You are clearly not in the mood, my friend. I'll email you some articles."

"Thank God," said Gwyn. "You're right. My head's not in the game. I promise to read everything you send me. With a highlighter in my hand. Which I promise to use. And when you see me on Saturday, I'll be an encyclopedia of Eugenics trivia."

"Okay, okay; I believe you. So what did you want to show me?"

"Oh," she said, taking another mouthful of pizza. "Right!" She stood up, walked over to a bookshelf stuffed with scrapbooks, and pulled one down. "Don't tell Ma I touched one of these while eating. She's a little obsessed. And don't get any food on the cover."

"Who's obsessed?"

"Shut up. She'll blame me, is all." She flipped past five or six pages. "Here." She pointed to a picture of our first grade classroom during a Halloween party. I saw me in my Princess Jasmine costume, with white long johns underneath because Mom wouldn't let me go out bare-bellied. I was clutching an enormous stuffed tiger.

She pointed to a picture of herself in a blonde wig as Cinderella. "Look at me being all Caucasian. And you trying to look Asian."

"Jasmine's *Middle-Eastern*, dweeb," I said.

Gwyn shrugged. "Whatever. Rajah there looks like he's big enough to eat you whole." She giggled. "So, you haven't always had it in for cats."

"Cats are fine," I said. I was really going to have to make it up to her for not helping with the cat-house cleaning.

"I found some other pictures—from when your mom taught Art. Ma made a whole book of those Art classes. If you want to see them . . ." she drifted off.

"I'd love to." Then I added hesitantly, "But I might cry."

"Silly girl. As if I'm afraid of tears."

Looking at her gentle smile, I felt another wave of guilt.

Gwyn retrieved a different cloth-bound volume

from the book case. I opened the first page and saw my mom, beaming at us from the photo. My throat constricted.

We flipped through pictures for an hour. Gwyn brought a whole box of tissues over because I was such a wreck. I tried wiping off my mascara smudges, but I must have done a bad job, and Gwyn offered to help.

"Hold still," she said, gently dabbing under my eyes, along my jawline.

I winced when she ran the tissue over last Sunday's bruise. Even after five days, I still needed cover-up.

"Whoa, Sam!" Gwyn eyed me and then my bruise. "What's this all about?"

"Er—I—uh, smacked into a wall a week ago."

She saw the guilt written all over my face and misinterpreted it.

"Sam, girlfriend, did someone hurt you?" Her dark eyes pierced mine.

I looked down. "Of course not. Just me being clumsy."

"Mmm-hmm," she intoned, still inspecting the bruise.

I turned that side of my face away from her gaze. "Seriously."

She stared at me until I wanted to disappear. She sighed heavily and took one of my hands. "I want you to know you can talk to me. If you ever need someone, okay?"

I nodded, blinking back tears, wishing I could tell her the truth. "I should head home now."

She reached over and gave me a hug, and then she walked me down the stairs and around the alley to get my bike. Just before I kicked off, she reached in her pocket and handed me a tiny ceramic frog.

"I want you to have it," she said.

On one of the Saturday Art classes with Mom, we'd modeled clay frogs. I'd lost mine years ago, but I still remembered Mom's excitement each year when the frogs came out of hibernation and started croaking. I hugged Gwyn one more time and took off down Main Street blinking back tears.

Once I reached home, I stopped long enough to drop off my backpack and ask Sylvia when I should be home for dinner. She gave me just a half an hour, and I rushed through reapplying mascara and cover-up. Feeling something in my pocket, I reached in, pulled out the ceramic frog, and remembered Mom saying some toads could hibernate for three years. They'd wake up when it was time and go about their lives, no big deal that they'd missed a few years.

Crazy.

I looked down at the frog again, and a great and terrible thought came to me.

Excerpted from the private journal of Girard L'Inferne, approx. 1945

Private lesson, Test Subject: Helga

"*Tell me,*" I ask, "*why this particular weapon?*"

"*The rock is hard and sharp. We call that kind shin-biter. If you fall upon it, you bleed.*" She is sullen, defiant.

"*It is a stone from another world,*" I say, smiling. "*Strange stories are told of the powers of tobiasite.*" I drop the smile and ask, "*Did you mean to kill Karl?*"

Clearly she expects punishment, perhaps even death. "*He was mocking the Führer. He could not be allowed to cause the other children to join in.*"

I nod. "*Older persons than you underestimate the danger of permitting others to laugh at what is sacred.*" I pause. "*Helga, I must know. Did you intend that he die?*"

The girl's face shifts slightly. Her jaw clenches, as do her fists. She nods.

"*You know you cannot be permitted to remain here after such a crime.*"

The girl nods again.

"*What would you think of joining a special school? One that trains loyal girls and boys like yourself to protect the brave leaders of The Thousand Year Reich?*"

The girl looks up, eyes full of desire.

"*Would you work hard at such a school? Would you prove to me that I made the right decision in not sending you to prison for your offense?*"

"In such a school," she declares gravely, *"I would work harder than anyone else."*

-translation by G. Pfeffer

11

CORRESPONDENCE

I biked the mile to Will's home, bursting to share my idea with him, praying I'd find him alone. I couldn't bring it up around his sister until Will and I had a chance to talk it through.

To the side of the cabin, I saw Will and Mickie. She pitchforked through a compost of leaves, dirt, and what looked like old newspaper where I pulled up my bike. Frustrated that I wouldn't have Will to myself, I braked too hard and my tires shimmied in the dirt. The air smelled a little like coffee. Rotten coffee. I wrinkled my nose and backed away.

"Give me a minute," Mickie said. "I'm feeding my compost. Bridget gave me twenty pounds of coffee grounds today." She grinned broadly. "Wish I'd thought to ask sooner." Her enthusiasm as she dug must have offered protection to her nasal passages. Why did everyone I know have smelly jobs?

Leaning my bike against the wall, I felt sweat dripping off me. The air felt like an oven, and I'd been pushing hard to get here fast. Mickie turned in time to see me using the neckline of my tee to dry the sweat from my face.

"Thank you for coming," Mickie said. "Will, take Sam inside. She needs some ice water. I'll be right in."

I followed Will towards the back door of the cabin, and he rippled.

"He's showing off," Mickie said, eyes rolling.

I laughed.

"Or maybe I didn't unlock that door yet." She shrugged.

A solidified Will unlocked the door from inside and I stepped in.

"Wait up," Mickie called, "I'm done."

She kicked off her compost-scented boots and joined us. "Sit by the fan," she said, adjusting the fan to blow straight on my face.

"You don't have to—"

She cut me off. "Your face is beet-red." She handed me the glass of chilled water. "Drink this. You're as bad as Will. People get *heat exhaustion* in weather like this."

I grinned, gulping my drink. I decided against mentioning that I'd lived my whole life in weather like this.

To the side of the desk, Will picked up and fished inside a large white envelope inscribed with calligraphy. He handed the letter to me.

Chère Mlle Baker,

I have put much thought into why Pfeffer chose to leave you in ignorance of the map with which he entrusted you. I can only conclude that he believed you would be safer if you did not know certain things—things which are indeed dangerous to know. Take it as a sign of how highly he valued your safety, although this is an area in which we disagreed. I believe you can be safer with knowledge than without it. However, lest this letter should fall into the wrong hands, I shall limit what I reveal as well. Please forgive me if I instead pose for you a series of riddles.

1: In who at *elements are each of the areas marked on the map rich?*

2: Have you heard of the curious effects such things as lead or quicksilver can have upon human health?

3: Begging you to pardon my indelicacy: do you know where your brother was conceived?

I shall, of course, be glad to provide a more thorough explanation of the map in person, should that someday prove a possibility. I regret that I am much occupied at present.

"So, any idea what all those riddles mean?" I asked.

"The answers are easy enough," Mickie said, shrugging. "Number one: gold and that whatsitmeteorite. Tobiasite? Number two: you get sick. Number three: Shelokum Hot Springs in Alaska."

Will groaned. "Geez, Mick!"

I gasped. I could feel color leaving my face. Before Mom died, I was often referred to as the "Bella Fria Hot Springs Surprise." I didn't know enough back then to be embarrassed, and it never came up after Dad remarried Sylvia.

Mickie looked at me intensely. "You didn't get your start at Shelokum too, did you?"

"Okay, that's enough," said Will. He stood and marched out the back door, slamming it shut.

My cheeks burned as I explained what I knew of my own conception to Mickie.

"I wonder how important the hot springs connection is . . . oh, this is crazy! Why didn't Pfeffer trust me enough to tell me what he knew? To explain those friggin' red dots?" She stood and paced. "That could be it, though. The presence of gold and tobiasite in a mineral hot springs at the time of conception. That could be what messes with the genetic code and produces the abnormalities we see in Helmann's carriers . . ."

"So your map marks the places around the world where Helmann's carriers are most likely to be, er—"

"Conceived," said Mickie. "That seems to be Sir Walter's answer."

"But there must be a hundred dots on those maps."

"Fifty-four," Mickie said. "But there's something that doesn't fit. Pfeffer once said that Will wouldn't be who he was if not for our dad's violence. When I asked what he meant, Pfeffer brushed it off and changed the topic."

"Maybe he just meant your dad helped form Will's character," I suggested.

"No, we were definitely talking about Will's ability to ripple. Maybe Pfeffer was purposefully trying to throw me off the trail. I'm going to have to meet with Sir Walter if I want answers." She crossed to her desk and began shuffling through papers. "Where is that flyer from French Club about chaperones?"

"I should get home for dinner," I said. "Tell Will I said 'bye.'"

Mickie nodded, clearly lost in thought, and I let myself out of the cabin.

Will stood outside, throwing rocks across the highway.

"Hey," I said, walking my bike over to him. "Can you come by tonight? I have something you need to hear about. It's important."

"Sure."

"Nine o'clock. The sliding glass door in back. No knocking—no door bells."

"No problem, rebel," he said, winking at me.

I kicked off on my bike and then hollered over my shoulder. "Talk to your sister about what she just figured out."

I heard Will groan as I sped away.

Predictably, Dad and Syl headed upstairs to watch TV in their room right before 9:00 and asked me to turn out the lights when I went to bed.

I walked around the quiet house, locking doors and turning off lights. I left the kitchen lights on and slipped outside to wait for Will. It was a clear night; the Big and Little Dippers shone brilliant overhead, but the air felt stuffy. Leaning against the house, I debated whether I should wait inside, but I decided I'd be cool enough if I got away from the heat radiating off the stucco walls.

I sat down in one of the lounge chairs. It felt surprisingly cooler. Would Will think my Big Idea was No Big Deal? Or had he already thought about my idea before? It was funny how the ceramic frog had driven my "aha" moment rather than Mr. Polwen's discussion of adaptations in biology this past week. I could still picture my notes from class.

Creatures hibernate to survive extreme cold.

At that moment, Will shimmered into view in front of me. I flew out of my seat, startled.

"Hey, Sam, hope I didn't scare you."

"Does a coronary count?" I asked.

"Sorry. I got here maybe a minute before you. I forgot I wasn't solid until you came out and you didn't see me."

"You ripple a lot, don't you?"

Will shrugged. "It saves time."

"You have no idea how loaded that statement is considering what I want to talk over with you."

"Hey, can I ask you a weird question first?"

"Be my guest," I said, wondering what other kind of question either of us would have.

"What were you thinking about, this second?"

I struggled to recall. "How warm it is tonight."

"Is that all you were thinking about?"

"I don't know. I guess. No, I was thinking about some note-taking I did in biology last week."

"Was this it: 'Creatures hibernate to survive extreme cold'?"

I stared at him, stunned. "Okay. Where. Did. That. Come. From?"

"From you, I think." His fingers caught in a tangle of curls as he scratched his head.

"How?"

"I'm not sure. When you came outside, just now, I was waiting in the lounge chair you sat down on."

I realized Will's 'presence' would account for the temperature. "It felt cold there."

"I bet it did."

My eyes dropped in embarrassment. I'd sat right on top of him.

"Okay, so here's what happened," Will said, unruffled. "Before I got up to ripple back solid, I saw a picture in my head of biology class, and the image was almost from the correct angle, but not quite, and then when the focus shifted down to my desk, I realized I was seeing your handwriting. It was like I was watching a video in my head, from your perspective."

I thought of the day at Illilouette Creek, the movie-like image in my mind's eye of a teenage girl with dark hair, hands on her hips, pointing to an ambulance, and shouting angrily. "I think this has happened to *me* before."

"Seriously?"

"Did your sister ever blame you for something to do with an ambulance? When she was maybe thirteen or fourteen?"

The deck was lit only by the light spilling through the sliding glass door, but even so, I could see Will's face turn pale. "The day I rippled for the first and only time in front of Mom. She called the hospital, thinking she was losing her mind. They sent an ambulance because Mickie couldn't drive yet. Mick was *furious* with me."

I brought my hand to my lips, feeling awful for bringing back the memory.

"I haven't thought about that since . . ."

"The day at Illilouette Creek," I finished in a whisper.

He locked eyes with me.

"You saw me remembering it that day?"

I nodded.

He whistled long and low. "We can read each other's minds."

I shifted nervously. I didn't want Will inside my head at this point in our friendship.

"Can you tell what I'm thinking right now?" he asked. I thought he looked anxious, but maybe that was my imagination.

"I don't think it works that way," I said. "I've only *seen* things when I was invisible. And I'm pretty sure we have to be touching as well. Like when I, um, sat through you just now."

He grinned. "Mickie would be so proud of you for that hypothesis."

I hoped he wasn't going to suggest we test the hypothesis. I couldn't let Will read my mind. "Have you ever, you know, read my mind before?" I asked.

"If this had ever happened before, I think it would have caught my attention."

I nodded, thinking of a way to distract him from suggesting we experiment in mind-reading. "Do you want to come in for cheesecake? We'd have to be quiet."

"Did your step-mom make it?"

I nodded.

He smiled. "Okay, now you're really reading my mind."

I stood up, opening the sliding glass door.

Will winked, rippled, and reappeared on the other side of the door, beaming. "Totally sick!" he whispered.

"Show off," I muttered, smiling. I opened the refrigerator, pulling out the cheesecake.

"You tried it yet, on your own?" He gestured to the glass.

"No. I've been meaning to since watching how you move around in your house, but I'm not alone much here."

He dug into the cheesecake I'd plated up for him. I grabbed myself a slice. Will gestured to the sliding glass door. "So, you up for an experiment? Trying glass?"

I smiled, glad he didn't mean a mind-reading experiment. Maybe he felt the same sort of caution I did, a hesitation to let someone so much inside you.

It only took moments before I was able to fade by thinking of the waterfall feature splashing down into our pool—a favorite watery image of mine. I smiled proudly in Will's direction, even though he couldn't see it, and I crossed to the door.

Passing through glass wasn't like anything else I'd experienced. It felt warm and viscous, forming itself into a second skin around me, then gently releasing me as I glided through to air again. A strong scent or taste reminded me of the beach, as well. Not the ocean-tang of the beach, but the sand itself. In geology, we'd learned that glass was silicon—sand. I ghosted back and forth several times, shivering through the viscous embrace before I rippled solid again.

"That is completely *amazing!*" I said.

"Did you know glass is actually a liquid that moves very, very slowly? That's what creates the distortions you can see on old glass, like Bridget's windows. I've never passed through those, though," he said, looking as if he meant to try. "So, what did you need to talk to me about?" Will looked at me, curious, as he plowed through a second slice of cheesecake.

"Oh, right!" *Mind-reading* had completely distracted my thoughts. "I had this idea today. About how hibernation and what we do are similar."

Will raised his eyebrows. "Never thought of that. You mean like how we don't get hungry or thirsty when we ripple?"

"There's obvious differences, though. I think with hibernating, you'd feel, well, asleep," I said.

"I feel *extra*-alive when I ripple, if anything."

"Same here. But I was actually going a different direction with the hibernating thing. What do you think would happen if you rippled for a year, or two years?"

"You mean, what would happen to me when I came back?"

"You wouldn't age, would you?" *Could he see where I was going with this?*

"I guess not. I mean, that's pretty much why Mickie thinks I took so long to, well you know, grow up. It's why I look younger than a normal eighteen-year-old."

Will flushed.

"So if someone carbon-dated you, you might only be fourteen or fifteen."

He shrugged. "Yeah, I guess so. This means you're several hours short of your calendar age too, huh?" He grabbed another bite and swallowed. Then he looked up at me and spoke a monosyllable softly. "Oh." Then, bigger. "*OH*." We locked eyes.

"The two of us could live a very long time, by spending part of every day invisible. If we wanted to." My voice came out just above a whisper. "So would you want to?"

"Live longer? I don't know, Sam. Sure, I guess. I mean, it's only in theory, anyway, right?"

"Yeah. It might not work like that." A really long life would be amazing if I got to pick who I lived it with. But I didn't say that. I couldn't be the one to say it, in case I was the only one feeling it. "You'll have to tell your sister. I wanted to tell you about it first, though."

"Yeah. She might not see it as the greatest news."

I nodded. "That's why I asked you to come over alone."

I wanted to sit and talk with Will all night, but my traitorous mouth kept yawning.

"I need to go before you fall asleep sitting here," said Will.

"It's like you read my mind," I joked sleepily.

"That's gonna get old, fast," he laughed. "Hey, you

want to get in some early morning running before practice starts? We could bike in early and then run the trails. We've got another round of hot weather coming."

"Sure," I said, my mouth pulling into a ginormous yawn.

"Goodnight, Sam." He rippled, passed through the glass door, and rippled back on the other side shooting me a double thumbs up before he took off running home.

***

The following day, Will came by early, but we'd both slept poorly with so much to think about, and Will admitted he was too tired for extra miles. But he wasn't too tired to meet early with me, I noted. I felt warm inside.

We strolled down to my childhood lookout to talk.

"I got another look at that little black book," Will said. "Mick had it sitting out last night. She was busy obsessing over Pfeffer's red-dotted maps. Anyway, I tried using an online translator, and it's not any language I can find."

"Not Latin after all?"

"No. Not Italian, Portuguese or Romanian either."

"We need to keep looking for a translation."

"Yeah. What with all the words looking like French or Spanish, I thought I was onto something trying

Italian."

"Hey—Italy—that reminds me. Gwyn says you make great pizza and asked if you could make it tomorrow? For the biology paper study session?"

"I'd forgotten that was tomorrow. Sure. It will be a good bribe to get Mick to help us on the research."

"Your sister loves pizza?"

"Mick's been on me about how she's got all these tomatoes that need to be used up, but I don't like making sauce in the cabin in this weather. However," he grinned hugely, "seeing as you have air-conditioning, that won't be an issue."

"How'd you learn? To make pizza?"

"School."

"Really?"

"I attended an alternative school. We had to volunteer a couple hours a week. I got good at pizza. I even got jobs catering because of my wicked crust."

"I wish you'd open a pizza place in Las Abs. You should advertise your talent."

Will shrugged. "Last year I was already a geek with being small and being a new kid. You throw in cooking and I don't think I could have survived the teasing."

I smiled. "So now that you're all buff you can admit to being an iron chef, huh?"

He flushed. "And *this* would be why I keep a lid on it."

"I think it's cool you can cook. Seriously cool."

It was time to take off for practice, but neither of us wanted to be the one to say, "Let's go." Instead, we spent a few minutes more drinking in the cool of the morning, watching hawks circle over the canyon.

Finally Will stood up, smiling at me. "You're going to love my pizza!"

Yeah.

Because I *so* needed things to love about Will.

Excerpted from the private journal of Girard L'Inferne, approx. 1943

The hungry boy sits upon his cot, his back to the corner, waiting for whatever might appear from behind the sealed door. Night approaches. Soon the meager light leaking into the room will be gone. He is not afraid, exactly; his emotions run more towards anger, or at times, desire. He knows he can endure more pain than any of the other children, and that without crying. This gives him a sense of his own superiority which serves to feed him when food is scarce. He does not mind being placed apart from the others; he despises them. There is only one person whom the hungry boy does not despise.

If he could order the world according to his liking, I would remain at his side, perhaps an advisor, maybe a servant. Amusing, the things he whispers into the dark when he thinks himself alone.

The door opens and the boy rouses himself, ready to fight or run.

"Hansi," I whisper. I carry a single candle—more than enough light for the boy to see and recognize me and the food I bring.

"I'm sorry it's been so long," I tell him. "I haven't been able to get away until now. Here." I hand a basket to the boy, pulling back the cloth covering the food. "My lunch and dinner. I do not need it as much as you, my young one."

The boy twists his mouth into something of a smile, with nothing of friendliness in it. "I knew you would come," he says as he chews through a large mouthful. "You come every tenth day."

"Do I, indeed?" My visits are, in fact, spaced in ten day intervals. This is the first time a secluded child has noticed. Hans is special. Intelligent, brave, a leader. "I wish I could do more for you. I don't need half the food I am given, but most days, it would be noted if I tried to steal away with it." He does not recognize that I lie. He has no idea of my pre-eminence in this laboratory.

"You are like me," says the boy. "I can go hungry without complaint as well. That's why you bring food to me, isn't it? Because I am so much better than the other schwein."

I cannot help smiling. "You are special. But you must never mention me to the other children. One word from any of them to my superiors, and that would be the end of the meals I bring for you."

"I can keep secrets," says the boy.

"Some day, perhaps, I can do more for you," I say, clapping the boy's shoulder.

The boy smiles. He is not capable of giving love—of that I have made sure, but he can feel its cousin, gratitude. His burden of indebtedness grows great, indeed.

-translation by G. Pfeffer

12

PIZZA AND PANNING

On Saturday morning, Will and Mickie showed up at my house an hour ahead of Gwyn, who was gathering gold panning pledges for the event on Monday.

Will carried a heavy-looking box of tools and ingredients, setting them on the kitchen stand. "Can Mickie use your high-speed to play around on Google Earth?"

Mickie carried in a tub of very ripe tomatoes. "I want to confirm the red dots mean hot springs, but our internet's been down."

"Back this way." *As if* I minded spending time alone with Will. By the time I'd gotten Mickie connected on Sylvia's computer, Will had already started in on the tomatoes, peeling and seeding them.

"Making a salad?" I asked, planting myself on a

barstool across from Will and the tomato pile.

"*We* are making the world's best pizza sauce. Do you know how to mince?"

"What, like with a knife?"

"Yeah."

"No."

"How about peeling carrots?" He rolled one my direction. "And garlic."

I knew how to peel a carrot. "Garlic makes sense for pizza sauce, but why the carrot?"

"It tones down acidity. You mince it so fine you can't even see it in the sauce."

"You mean *you* mince it," I said, passing him a peeled carrot.

"Come over here," he said. As I walked around the island to him, he sliced the carrot in half lengthwise and placed the halves flat-side-down on the cutting board. "Mincing is a simple action. Here." He placed his hand over the top of mine, showing me how to curl my fingers under so I wouldn't accidentally cut off my fingertips. Then he showed me how to rock the blade, keeping the tip anchored to the board as we knifed through the carrots. It was awkward to do this side by side.

"Hang on," he said.

He moved behind me to bring an arm around me on either side. Warmth hummed between our bodies, and I shivered as he closed in, reaching once more for my hand over the knife.

I let it slip at exactly the wrong moment. Staring stupidly, I watched a blossom of red spreading across Will's knuckles just as Mickie wandered in.

"Oops," said Will, noticing the cut.

"That's what you get for moving in on a girl's personal space like that," Mickie muttered as she grabbed a paper towel, pressing it on her brother's hand. "You got Band-Aids?"

"Yeah," I said. "I'll be right back." I slipped away from Will's arms and raced upstairs to my bathroom. "Idiot, idiot, idiot," I whispered as I grabbed polysporin and Band-Aids, and then sprinted back down to the kitchen.

"I'm so sorry," I said, handing the box to Will. "Does it hurt badly?"

"Can't even feel it," he said, smiling.

Mickie gathered up the bits of Band-Aid wrappings and paper towel, grunting, "Trashcan?"

"In the pantry," I said, pointing to the far side of the room.

"Didn't mean to cross any lines, there," Will murmured, too low for Mickie to hear.

I stared, wanting to communicate he shouldn't be embarrassed, that he didn't need to say anything. That if he would fall in love with me, he wouldn't have to worry about crossing lines.

Of course I couldn't say any of that.

"Where's the oregano?" Will asked his sister. He threw the minced carrots and all of the tomatoes into a sturdy looking pot on the front burner.

"You didn't say oregano," she replied.

"I *specifically* said we needed oregano."

"You said basil."

"*And* oregano."

I jumped in. "I think Sylvia grows it in the herb bed if you need fresh."

They looked at me as if suddenly remembering I was in the room, and Will chortled.

"I don't exactly know what it looks like," I admitted. "And Syl's out this morning."

"I'll go," Mickie said, a peace-making gesture.

Will passed a basil plant to me, picking up where we'd left off like nothing awkward had happened. "Chop some basil," he said.

I winced at the word "chop," but he passed me a pair of kitchen shears. "Snip the leaves in this bowl over and over 'til they're super-tiny."

"Yes, Chef. Right away, Chef." I grinned.

He threw a potholder at me, then minced the garlic and tossed it in oil.

"So you catered for people—making pizza?" I asked.

"Graduation parties, a bat-mitzvah, a fundraiser for a deaf parenting organization. That one was messy," he laughed, "me trying to cook and sign—there's like,

171

cheese and sauce flying everywhere."

"You sign?" I asked.

Mickie re-entered with a fragrant handful of oregano stems.

"Yeah, some."

"He's fluent," said Mickie. "Plus he had two years of Spanish, right *mi hermoso?* So he can spout like an idiot in three languages."

"Tri-lingual? No wonder you're so good at French."

"Not as good as you," he shrugged. "But I like words. Got that from my mom. She was learning to sign so she could interpret in classrooms. She would come home from her lessons, and she'd teach me because it made her learn better."

"Your step-mom's garden is amazing," said Mickie. "I need her to tell me how to grow berries in this climate. Mine didn't make it through the winter."

"Sylvia can talk berries with you all day," I said, grinning. "By the way, thanks for sharing your garden tomatoes—I hope you're not using them all up today."

Will barked out a laugh.

"There's way too many for us this year," Mickie said. "Plus, now I get to enjoy some of my little brother's fresh tomato sauce. He won't make it when it's just us. This is a major honor he's bestowing here."

I looked at Will, who was busy dumping basil into the sauce. I thought I saw his face redden.

"Will's not actually letting you help, is he? He doesn't let anyone near him in the kitchen, usually."

A smile spread across my face.

Will's mouth turned up slightly at the corners. "I don't let *you* anywhere near me in the kitchen, Mick."

"Can you come stir, Sam?" Will asked. "I need to rescue the garlic."

I grabbed the bamboo spoon, buttery-smooth against my palm and warm from where he'd held it. Will added slivers of nutty-bright-scented garlic. My stomach growled.

He gestured for me to hand him the stirring spoon, and our fingers tangled as I passed it. He grinned at me and blew on the sauce, then put his lips to the spoon and sucked in a teeny taste.

"Try this." He guided the spoon carefully to my mouth. "Blow on it first," he cautioned.

I blew, but not gently enough, and sauce pushed across onto his fingers. I giggled and then tried a taste from the spoon.

"What do you think?" Will asked.

I watched as he licked the sauce off his fingers. "Intoxicating." I felt my skin warming. "You missed some." I tapped the side of my mouth to demonstrate where.

He tongue moved alongside his mouth.

I swallowed. "Wrong side." I pointed again, touched his face.

"You missed some too, unless you're saving that for later." Will gently swiped around my mouth. I blushed five shades of red and turned away as the doorbell rang.

Gwyn.

Will turned to grab the dough and I let Gwyn inside.

"Omigod!" she said. "It smells like I've died and gone to pizza-heaven." She flopped dramatically into a barstool on my side of the kitchen island. "Well, I think I've visited every business in greater Las Abuelitas, and I'm up to two-hundred and five bucks an hour. With numbers like that, who cares if I find gold?"

"Wow." I seriously hoped she wouldn't ask where my pledge total stood at the moment. I'd been meaning to call my grandma and hit up my folks. I just hadn't done it yet.

Gwyn pulled a stack of papers from her purse and set them on the counter. "Possible additions to our research."

Mickie glanced over Gwyn's printouts. She pointed to two of them, "You'll never find enough on these . . ."

I stood up to let Mickie take my place where she could examine the topics more easily. Staring outside, I crossed to the sliding glass door; the *Panning for Felines* event was the day after tomorrow, and I still didn't feel confident that I could spend the whole day at the creek without rippling. My gut knotted. What if I failed?

There'd be camera-men from Oakhurst, followed by helicopters from Fresno, followed by the National Guard, and ending with me being kidnapped or killed. My heart hammered.

I needed to calm down.

I watched sunlight flickering upon our swimming pool. I took some deep breaths. From a few feet behind me, I heard my friends murmuring over our biology paper. I began to calm, looking at the water. The pool looked so inviting. I should have told everyone to bring swim stuff.

"Where's Sam?" asked Gwyn, interrupting my reverie.

I turned back towards my friends, pasted on a smile and began to move back towards the kitchen island. At which point I realized I was no longer solid; gliding invisibly felt entirely different from walking on the ground.

Crap. I can't even stay solid at my own house for five minutes.

How would I manage a day at Bella Fria creek? Will shot Mickie a meaning-filled glance. They knew what I'd done. I needed to go somewhere so that I could ripple back solid without Gwyn seeing it. I ghosted through the sliding glass door—delicious—and passed out of sight around the side of the house. After rematerializing, I flicked the waterfall switch—an excuse for having stepped out—then ran back to the sliding glass door and let myself in.

"Where'd you go?" Gwyn asked.

"I wanted to see if Dad got the waterfall fixed," I said.

"Focus, Sam, focus," said Gwyn. "Biology? What do you think of this for our final topic: Designer Babies: How Far is Too Far?"

"Uh, great," I said, splashing some cool water on my face. I returned to the kitchen island and rifled through the print-outs Gwyn had brought with her. One of them caught my eye and I skimmed through it.

It was disturbing.

"Sam?" asked Will. "You okay? You look a little pale."

I turned to Gwyn. "Did you read this one?"

"Girlfriend, I haven't read anything. Ma's been on my butt all week about the damned cat fundraiser."

"What's it say?" asked Will.

"It says that there was a state that sterilized tens of thousands of people *involuntarily* in the twentieth century. Any guesses which one?" I asked.

"Duh, Sam, Nazi Germany," said Gwyn.

"*California*," I said. "If you suffered from chronic depression, or had Autism, or if you were a lesbian, you could be locked up and sterilized *without* your consent as being unfit to reproduce."

"That's true," said Mickie.

"That's awful!" said Gwyn.

176

"Also true," said Mickie. "California was the perfect state for the idea of Eugenics to take hold. Farmers were making incredible discoveries in the twentieth century—breeding and cross-breeding that revolutionized crop yields. That same reasoning led the state of California to conclude it was justified in allowing the incarceration and involuntary sterilization of over thirty-thousand people."

I scanned through the rest of the article. "This says that during the Nuremberg Trials, Nazi officials who practiced their version of Eugenics cited the origin of the practice in the United States of America as a justification for what they had done."

"Wow, Sam, do you know how to pick a research topic or what?" asked Gwyn.

The rest of the afternoon passed in a blur. The article on Eugenics was troubling, but it wasn't immediate. I had other things to worry about. Like my inability to control my body. Like the fact that there was no way I could do the panning event and guarantee I'd stay solid. And how there was no way I could explain to Gwyn *why* I couldn't do the event.

***

The following morning arrived and the sky was gray and ominous, thunder rattling in the distance. I dreaded having to tell Gwyn I couldn't go panning at

Bella Fria Creek, but the event was tomorrow, Labor Day. So I had to tell her today. I dug through my sock drawer and found one-hundred-sixty-five dollars: a twenty-dollar-an-hour pledge. As though I could buy forgiveness.

Rain splattered against my window, the first storm of the season, and I pulled on sweats and a hoodie. Following the storm east towards the Sierra, I biked to Gwyn's, wallet bulging with my guilt offering. After parking my bike in front of the café, I walked around back and rang the buzzer.

Gwyn thumped down the stairs and opened the door. "Hey, Sam. Geez, you're soaked. I haven't had a minute to shower with this damn cat-a-thon. I should just step outside, huh?" She held her hand out in the rain for a moment, then withdrew it, climbing the stairs ahead of me. "There's a zillion details, and of course Ma can't do any of it that involves computers. How's your pledge sheet looking?"

I hesitated. My mouth felt stuck shut like I'd filled it with crazy-glue. I took a deep breath. "I can't do it."

"Huh?"

"Gold panning."

"What? Sam, what do you mean you can't do it? Did something else come up?"

I crossed to look out the window down over the cat houses. I didn't want to lie to her. "No," I said at last. "I just . . . can't."

"Are you grounded? No, of course not. You wouldn't be here. You're not sick are you? Omigod. Of course. I'm an idiot. It's your thing with cats, isn't it? You hate cats, only you're afraid to tell me."

"I don't hate cats."

"Hello. Do me the courtesy of being honest. You told me the story about your Mom's accident."

What had I told her? I didn't think I'd said I didn't like cats. "I didn't mean to imply I don't like them. Cats are fine."

"So what is it then?" She was puzzled and a little irritated.

I should have said it was cats.

"I don't really want to talk about it," I said. "I just came here to tell you in person that I won't be there. And to give you a pledge." I pulled out my wallet, grabbing at the wad inside. "It's enough for twenty dollars an hour."

Gwyn walked over, looked at the money, then at me. "You don't have to do this, Sam. I'd rather you'd just be honest. I'm okay if you don't like cats."

"It's not the damn cats!"

We stared at each other.

"Okay, whatever," she said coolly. "I need to grab a shower. It's going to be a long day."

She turned to go.

"I'm sorry," I said. I stood there, not wanting to leave.

"Uh-huh," she grunted, as she walked away. "Close the door tight when you leave."

Excerpted from the private journal of Girard L'Inferne, approx. 1943

Experiment 31, Control Group B

I tell Matron to replace the children's down comforters with woolen blankets, one for every two children. The matron murmurs she will clean the eiderdowns. I tell her the children must develop strength and endurance to serve their Fatherland, their Führer.

The children turn to bed that night as the ground freezes hard outside.

"Give me that bedspread!" shouts Helga, who has just discovered her blanket is gone.

"It's mine," says Elfie. She is small for her age. "It was put on my bed."

"Fight me for it," says Helga.

"No," replies Elfie. She knows Helga is a fierce opponent.

But the choice to avoid fighting is not available. Elfie will fight or she will give up the blanket. Helga grins, white teeth gleaming in the dark, cold night.

-translation by G. Pfeffer

13

COVER UP

I stared at my bike, in front of Las ABC. I didn't want to bike; I needed to run. What had I done to my friendship with Gwyn?

The weather had shifted again, from stormy to sultry. The hoodie had been a mistake, but not my biggest one today. My bike could wait; I needed to run.

I took off into the sticky morning, my feet carrying me up into the hills, along the 7K trail. Up through oak branches, leaves drooping with rain, up the patches slick with new mud. On and on until the ache eased in my chest, until the confrontation with Gwyn looked like something we could both move past.

This was why I ran. Because it was the only way I had to move through the pain of being alive to a space where it became bearable, seemed possible.

I ran on and on until my feet brought me back to Las ABC, and then I hopped on my bike without looking to find out if Gwyn or Bridget could see me.

At home, I was into my swimsuit in minutes. The pool glimmered invitingly, but in spite of the morning rain-shower, the water was right below bath-temperature. I felt restless in the pool, and soon I took off down the path to my lookout where I knew I could count on a breeze to pass over my wet, warm skin. On the way, I saw Sylvia, picking late raspberries and corn. She smiled and held out a handful of my favorite fruit. The raspberries were large, firm, and sweet with a hint of acid-tang that made them my favorite. I gleaned a few she'd missed, popping them in my mouth, too.

"First two weeks of school behind you, huh?" she asked softly.

"Yeah," I replied, pausing a moment beside her.

"So how are things going?"

"Classes are fine." I wanted to tell her more, but I didn't know how to explain my thing with Gwyn.

"School's a lot more than classes, huh? That's what I remember from the olden days." She passed me a couple more berries, and I sat beside her.

"That hasn't changed," I agreed.

"Things okay with you and your friends?" She was good at catching small shifts in my mood.

"Fine," I said. The half-truth pulled color to my face. "Well, sort of fine."

She waited, patient beside me, rustling through the vines for scarlet fruit.

"I don't know what I should do. I made Gwyn really mad at me, and I didn't mean to, and I can't figure out how to fix it." My eyes swilled with stinging tears.

"I thought maybe something was wrong, baby. So you're worried you won't be able to patch it up?"

I nodded, tears spilling onto my cheeks, salty as they trailed down past my lips. She passed me a paper-towel from the roll she was using to pad between layers of raspberries.

"You know you can tell me anything, right baby?"

No, I can't, I thought.

"What is it honey? Tell me."

"I can't," I said, my throat contracting as several more tears escaped.

Her eyes narrowed and she gazed out over the ravine, following birds that dove and swooped as if to celebrate the earlier rain. "Okay, then. So what do you think you should do, honey?"

"I need to apologi—ize," I said, my breath catching in a hiccup as I forced myself to stop crying.

"You are a very smart young woman. 'I'm sorry' goes a long way. You'll find a time when you can tell her, all by yourself. It's your first falling-out, right?"

I nodded.

"Ah, Sammy." Sylvia reached over and gathered me into a tender embrace, rubbing my shoulders and back.

"We only argue with the people we really care about. You girls are going to figure this out just fine." I let her hold me, feeling grateful and comforted.

"Is friendship always . . . this hard?" I asked in a whisper.

Sylvia laughed softly. "Only the friendships that are truly worthwhile."

I dabbed at my face, clearing away the salty tear-tracks left behind by the heat and breeze. I felt a little better.

Hunkering down beside one of the garden beds, I looked for stray weeds hiding among the raspberry canes. It was a small way I could show gratitude to my step-mom. Something up the path to the house caught my eye: Mickie.

Sylvia noticed her and called up a greeting. "Hi, Mackenzie! You finally made it!"

"It's been long enough, huh?" Mickie grinned that huge white smile I knew so well from seeing it on her brother's face. "This is wonderful," she said, pointing to the vista down the ravine.

Sylvia beamed.

"Hey Sam." Mickie smiled at me.

"Hey."

"I'm here to check out Sylvia's famous berries."

Sylvia straightened up, her knees and back popping. "Right. Let's go over to the far bed. Those are the boysen—well, the syllaberries," she said, making an effort to call them by their proper name. Dad had named them for her.

I remained quietly foraging for stray fruit as Sylvia and Mickie talked about the challenges of growing valley-bred syllaberries at our higher and colder climate.

When they said their goodbyes, Mickie turned to me. "We're taking off to Fresno early tomorrow for some shoe shopping. Las Abs is sold out of everything in a size eleven. Will thought you might have his hoodie? It's getting colder driving in the morning with the top off the Jeep."

"Uh, yeah, I've got it in my bedroom. So you guys are missing the cat fundraiser, too?" I asked, surprised.

"Crap." She frowned. "Guess we'll have to, 'cause no way am I letting Will wear out his new running shoes around school another week, and nothing else fits."

I understood. Good shoes for cross-country were a big expense, and they wore out fast enough without using them for everyday.

As we climbed up the railroad-tie stairs, I glanced over and recognized an expression on her face. I'd seen that look when Will concentrated.

"Will and I want to ask you something," she said. "Will says you know the French teacher pretty well? Old family friends?"

"She and my mom: they were friends."

"I have this book from my former advisor, Dr. Pfeffer. He thought it was important enough to send it to me right before he was murdered. I want to know what the book's about, but it's in some language I can't figure out."

I nodded.

"Anyway, I wondered if you might be willing to take a couple of sentences and ask the French teacher if she recognizes the language. I mean, Will could ask her—"

"Better to keep Will one additional step removed from the book and Dr. Pfeffer."

"Well, yeah, that's what I was thinking." She dropped her eyes, embarrassed.

"That's smart."

She looked up, gave me a sad smile, then pulled the book from her bag, and handed it to me. "It might not be anything. Anyway, the sentences translated into English are some pretty weird stuff. But Pfeffer thought it was important enough to send to my keeping."

"I'll let you know what I find out."

We paused at the sliding glass door.

"Thanks, Sam," she said. "I've worried about keeping Will safe so long, I don't know the reasonable fears from the far-fetched ones any more. When we were kids I had to keep what he could do hidden from Dad—not a good secret to share with an addict. Then I started worrying the CIA would haul Will off or he'd end up a lab-rat somewhere. And now with Pfeffer and the Helmann's carriers being killed . . ."

"I don't blame you. Not for a minute."

"Thanks," she said. Her mouth pulled into a sad half-smile. "So I bet Will loves this door," Mickie tapped the glass as she closed it behind us.

I nodded, smiling.

We reached my room and I grabbed the hoodie off my desk chair and passed it to her.

Mickie looked around my room. "Nice. Real home-y."

I saw a flash of yearning, but it disappeared quickly.

"Speaking of home, my brother gets steamed if he's got dinner done and I'm not there. Time to go."

I led her down to our front door, holding it opened.

"I'll be seeing you," she said.

"Bye, Mick." I watched as she walked out to her Jeep, my mind an astonished whirl. Mickie had just handed me a book that her brother said she wouldn't let him touch. A smile spread across my face. She trusted me.

I settled into my bean-bag chair and opened the book. The handwriting was cramped but neat. The individual letters were all part of the alphabet I knew, which meant it had to be European, and there weren't any strange additional letters or symbols like those from Germany or the Scandinavian countries. Will was right about Latin. Not enough "hic" or "hoc" or words ending in "ibus."

As I flipped through the pages, I noted short phrases scrawled in margins and once, on a page by itself:

Lisaba es partida.

Or sometimes:

Helisabat es partida.

And often:

Helisabat es morta.

I knew how to translate that one. *Helisabat is dead.*

Tuesday morning I asked Madame Evans about a couple of phrases I'd jotted down. Everyone else had filed out of the classroom. Gwyn hadn't spoken two words to me, and I hoped that was because she was exhausted after the Panning Event.

Madame puzzled over the phrases. "Where did you run across this writing?"

"An old journal." I didn't trust myself to create an elaborate lie.

"Your mom's side of the family, I take it?"

I made a noise that could be interpreted as agreement.

"I'm wondering if it's Cajun, because of your mom's Lousiana roots. See this: 'aver besonh de' sounds a lot like *avoir besoin de*, to have need of. And 'la rason perqué' is similar to *la raison pourquoi*, the reason why. Maybe the person who wrote this lacked the knowledge of proper spelling and simply gave his or her best guess.

This one, 'ne sabi pas res,' has the French *'ne pas'* structure, but the two other words are anyone's guess. 'Sabi' could be a corruption of *savoir*, I suppose: to know."

"So Cajun is French?" I asked.

"Cajun is a language in its own right, but its roots are French. We'll listen to some music and dialog in your third year French class. That's my best guess, *Samanthe*, with your mom's family history."

"Okay," I said. "Thanks a lot. *Merci beaucoup.*"

Of course my mom's background had nothing to do with this black book. Still, the idea of a *version* of French was a good one. There were moments when I felt like I could *almost* understand some of the sentences. We just had to find a language derived from French instead of from Latin, like Will and I had been thinking.

I didn't catch up with Gwyn to ask her how things had gone with the fundraiser that first day back. On Wednesday and Thursday, she remained cool towards me, and I began to worry this wouldn't blow over soon. I couldn't apologize because I couldn't catch her attention.

Will asked me what was wrong on Thursday.

"Gwyn hates me," I said glumly.

"Yeah, right."

"I'm serious. She thinks I hate cats, and that's why I didn't gold pan, and I told her I don't hate cats, and she thinks I'm lying to her." My throat tightened as I spoke.

"She didn't say anything to me about missing the fundraiser. Actually, she hasn't said anything to me all week. Maybe she's mad at both of us."

All too likely, I thought.

Friday, Will's sister was taking him to lunch. Eating alone was nothing new to me, but I wasn't going back to snarfing in the halls and hiding in the library like I used to. I walked towards a table where Gwyn sat, alone for the moment.

She looked up at me without smiling or frowning, scanning my face, looking for bruises or heavy layers of cover-up. She spoke first.

"Do you know what I see looking out our back window?"

"The cat kennels?" I guessed.

She looked away for a moment. "The night someone took a shot at the cats, I looked out and I thought I saw Will climbing over the back fence. Did he come for target practice on our cats?"

"What?" I didn't believe what she'd just asked.

"I'd really like to be friends, and I know Will's had some rough patches in his life. But I can't stand the dishonesty, Sam. He needs to get help for this kind of problem because it won't go away on its own. It'll get worse, Sam."

She didn't wait for me to respond.

"I didn't want to believe it—Will seems like such a nice guy—but all the clues line up in one direction. And there's his dad and all. Violent criminals often start with violence directed at animals."

"Will's not violent with animals or people." My voice was a whisper.

"Sam, you can get help. I saw the bruise, remember?"

I shook my head. "You've got it all wrong."

"Sam, I think you know the truth about Will. I think you were with Will that night. Am I right?"

I blinked frantically, but it did no good. Tears forced their way past my closed lids. I couldn't tell her the truth. But I couldn't lie either; she'd know if I did.

"You've got it all wrong," I choked out.

"You're a really bad liar." She shook her head. "You said you like that I give it to you straight. Well, this is me, giving it to you straight. I thought you were a lot smarter than this, Sam. No guy is worth this. I can forgive a lot of things, but lying and abuse are two things I won't tolerate." She stood up. "And neither should you." She left the table.

I heard big, gulping sobs coming from somewhere. From me. I ran to the track where I cried with abandon.

***

Sylvia asked me the next morning what was wrong.

I wanted to tell her the truth. But I just said I needed to be alone. When I went outside, she didn't hover. There are times I want to put this woman up for saint-hood.

Wandering to the far side of the deck, I stared across the pool at the waterfall, but it had no power to soothe me. I could have Gwyn as my friend, or Will, but not both. Gwyn would continue to cold-shoulder me unless I explained what had really happened that night. But Will and his sister would leave town if I told anyone about rippling. And that meant letting Gwyn believe I was in an abusive relationship with a guy who tortured cats for fun. That's what this came down to. I had to choose who I could bear to live without.

For about an hour, I considered lying to Gwyn. Saying that I had a thing for shooting critters, and that I knew I needed help and would she point me to a twelve-step program for cat-haters? I saw myself in a room full of people confessing to terrible compulsions, all encouraging each other to take that energy and build squirrel feeders instead.

But I couldn't lie my way out of a paper bag, and Gwyn knew it.

So who could I live without? At the moment, I was experiencing life without Gwyn. It sucked. Sure I had Syl, but she was a mom, not a girlfriend. Mickie was my friend, and a girl, but it wasn't the same.

Life without Gwyn.

I felt a lump forming in the back of my throat.

But if I told Gwyn the truth?

Life without Will.

His sister would take him away, and I'd never see him again. Will punching me on the shoulder like I was his best friend. Will holding me safe in the creek, bringing me back to safety and life. Will and his grin aimed straight at me, his eyes crinkling as he smiled, so he looked sleepy and sexy at the same time.

Life without Will.

I couldn't breathe.

I tasted all the bitterness of this choice, because if life were fair, I wouldn't have to choose between them. But life is never about fair.

Excerpted from the private journal of Girard L'Inferne, approx. 1943

Indebtedness Training—Test Subject: Helga

"It isn't fair," the girl whispers. "I should have been chosen. I am stronger and smarter than Greta."

"Never mind, Helga," I say. "If the couple wanted a child like Greta, they would not, I think, have made good parents for someone as exceptional as you."

She does not know that I release only the children I consider failures, so she nods.

"Eat, child. I saved my lunch and dinner for you. I wish it could be more." I am lying, but the child does not know. "Perhaps someday I will find a nice Fraulein to marry, and we will adopt you."

"You would make a good father. Life is not always fair, I think," says the child, seeming to find comfort in the idea as much as in the food.

"No, child, hardly ever," I agree.

She smiles with a new thought. "If everything were fair, I would not get extra food from you either."

I smile back, happy at the increased burden of indebtedness the girl feels with each of these visits.

-translation by G. Pfeffer

14

BLISS

Weeks flowed by and school settled into a routine for me, my academic work off-set by cross country practice. Our teams had never filled out in numbers enough to compete, but I didn't mind. Meets just didn't matter, in light of other things. I missed Gwyn's friendship, and running on the same team only made the space between us more painful. The end of the month loomed ahead—on October 27th I would turn sixteen. Gwyn and I had talked about celebrating this milestone at Las ABC with lots of caffeine and sugar. But that part of turning sixteen wouldn't be happening now.

I sat outside, down at my lookout, gathering the last bit of October sunshine. Below and to the west, the Valley lay smothered in a blanket of tule fog. Soon it would be too cold to sit here, even in the afternoons. I thought about getting up, and then I heard someone coming my direction, which basically never happens. I looked and saw Will flashing a hundred-watt grin my direction.

"Sylvia said you might be down here." He was holding a plastic baggy stuffed with something green. "It's basil. Mick wants a celebratory dinner tonight. Pesto's the only thing she knows how to make from scratch. So she called your step-mom and here I am."

"What are you celebrating?"

"We found out today that our dad got arrested last June. Two counts of possession and resisting arrest." Will smiled. No, he glowed. His hair had grown, untrimmed, for several months now. It suited him, dark curls framing that bright face.

"And that's a good thing?"

"A very good thing." As he said this, his grin changed and looked almost feral. "He's got a year in drug court."

I stared in fascination at the animal expression of his mouth.

"So, yeah, today's a very good day." His smile relaxed, back into a comfortable grin.

I'd wanted to ask questions about his dad for a long time. "You said he started using to cure his Helmann's or something?"

His brow contracted.

"We totally don't have to talk about this if you don't want to," I said.

"'S'okay." He looked at his watch and sat on a stump beside me. "I got a few minutes. The Neuroprine, the Helmann's drug, it kept him from going numb at inconvenient times, but it had a few side effects. Stuff like drowsiness, loss of appetite and, uh, *libido*." He spoke the word like it might bite him. "Parent" and "sex drive" are *so* not meant to be thought of at the same time.

Will continued. "For a long time the side effects didn't bother him. I mean, he was a kid, right? But this doctor mentioned one visit that before the prescription existed, people would sometimes self-medicate with controlled substances, which didn't have the side effects—uh—like I mentioned. Obviously they had other side effects, though, like being illegal and making you crazy. The doctor must have meant to tell Dad how lucky he was to live in an age with a safer option. But that wasn't what my dad did with the information.

"Dad meets my mom in Thailand doing Peace Corps, and he's all in love with her, and he starts thinking maybe an alternative drug is a better idea, and that's when he started using. Mom was pissed when she found out."

"Wow. I had no idea your parents did Peace Corps."

"Yeah, go figure, huh? I never got to see that side

of my dad. It took Mom a long time to give up hoping it would return." Will shook the bag of basil and seemed to decide it was time to change the subject. "You and Gwyn figured things out yet?"

"We're not friends anymore."

"Serious?"

I nodded.

"Why?"

I sighed, kicking my feet out in front of me. "She's convinced you came to her place to shoot cats the night I blew that hole in the wall. And that I basically gave you my blessing, by not stopping you."

Will laughed. "For real? That's hysterical!" He looked over at me and his grin faded. "I'll go over right now and set Gwyn straight it wasn't like that."

I shook my head. "I don't think that's a good idea."

"It's not like I'll tell her what really happened."

"It isn't that." I struggled to find the right words. "Gwyn thinks . . . it's just . . . with your dad and all . . ."

"You can tell me." Face stoic, he gazed out across the canyon. "I'm used to the kinds of things people think once they hear about my dad."

"You know how I had those bruises, from where the rocks hit my face?" I glanced over to catch his expression. "She thinks," I paused; my voice dropped to a murmur. "She thinks you beat me. And she thinks that I'm okay with it."

I watched as the muscles on the side of Will's jaw

clenched. "Geez." He scuffed at the dirt with his heel and stared out across the Valley. "Didn't see that one coming."

The sun snuck behind a low wall of clouds and the temperature fell a couple of degrees. I shivered.

"And of course I'm not going to tell her the truth," I said. "Because then I'd lose you, too. I've seen how fast Mickie can pack up a house."

He looked at me as if to ask a question, but no words came out. I dropped my gaze, confused by the intensity of his. A breeze passed over us, whispering of icy weather to come. Will ran an arm around my shoulder. For comfort? For the cold?

"She's observant, though." Will's voice was low and rough.

I turned to meet his eyes. "Observant? About . . . ?"

He dropped the basil and brought his other hand over onto mine, tracing the tops of my fingers with his own. I forgot about the cold. My entire world focused down to the space where his skin touched mine.

And I understood.

Will angled his face closer to mine. His cheeks were flushed, his dark eyes bottomless wells in which worlds could be lost. He wasn't in a hurry and although I wanted his kiss more than I'd ever wanted anything, I didn't rush either. Did I know how to kiss a boy? I wanted to kiss this boy right. So I hovered, and he hovered, and we inhaled each other's shallow breaths, warm and sweet and salty with desire, and then when I knew I couldn't stand it anymore, he leaned in a millimeter closer, like a runner trying to be first through the ribbon.

His lips touched mine. Soft and yielding, chapped on one side, tasting like every good thing. I felt his inhalations, soft and fast against my upper-lip, and heat spread out from my heart, undulating along my torso and through my arms and legs, fingers and toes, and me feeling better than running at sunrise.

My cell *thunked* out of my pocket onto the dirt, and we pulled apart for a brief moment, locked in each other's gaze. Then like gravity, or maybe like magnets, our lips met again because they had to. And in that touch it felt like I was buried treasure he'd crossed seven seas to claim. I couldn't feel the edges of my own body anymore; I was melting into his.

Oh.

I *had* melted. I'd rippled.

My phone vibed loudly at Will's solid feet. He reached down and grabbed it.

"It's my sister calling you. I'm gonna answer, okay?"

I nodded, then realized he couldn't see me. I stood and moved a few feet away and rippled back solid. Will stood as well and was nodding, listening to his sister and grunting a series of assents. He clicked off. "That was

Mickie."

"Yeah," I said, back in my body.

"She's says my butt's in a sling if I don't get back home five minutes ago. For our dinner thing."

We began the walk back through the garden, neither of us speaking. We passed through the house and to the drive. Will paused a moment before his sister's Jeep. "It's okay if you don't feel that way. I just want us to be friends no matter what, okay?"

I couldn't find the words to answer, so I leaned in and kissed him on the cheek, hoping that reassured him.

"Right," he said, all flushed. He climbed in the Jeep and started the engine. "See you tomorrow."

"Hey!" I called out.

Will stopped, leaning his head out the window.

"My birthday's next Saturday. Come over with your sister for chocolate cake and a bonfire. It's our tradition. It's how we get rid of the burn pile every fall." I hoped it didn't sound lame.

"We'll be there," Will said as he took off, waving.

That night, I picked the black book up again. I'd left off trying to translate it for a couple of weeks because what little I could understand sounded pretty horrible. I settled down to attempt additional translation from where I'd left off.

Fam es le compan qui coljare amb les enfans cada noit.

"Hunger is the companion who—" and then

something "the children" something "night." I thought back to the "math puzzles" where the children didn't have enough food. So maybe, "Hunger is the children's companion at night?"

With this frustrating method of translation, I was confirming what Will and I had suspected: the puzzles listed in English at the beginning of the book had actually been carried out as experiments.

I wanted to think of these children and their situations as imaginary, but I knew somehow they were real. I wanted to say I'd never find myself in such a situation, but if Mickie was right, there were those who wanted me dead or available for experimentation, too.

I didn't want to think about hiding and suffering, about how long we could stay safe: me and Mickie and Will. I wanted to remember Will's kiss—to hold it close and bathe the world in its glow. I set the book down.

That night I dreamed of Will. I was his cross-country partner, our feet beating out a rhythm on hot pavement beneath a blistering sun. This rhythm, Will running at my side, became the cadence to which my heart beat. Then we were small children and he was chasing me through piles of autumn leaves at the park. At last I was his lover, and I pressed him to my heart while snow fell silently around us. I sat up, suddenly awake in the soundless dark of a chill morning.

Excerpted from the private journal of Girard L'Inferne, approx. 1943

Experiment 56, control group C

Hunger is the companion who lies with the children nightly, calling them to rise every dawn.

But thirst? The children have not yet encountered this newest adversary.

To one side of the room, a basin rests upon a small table. Light from the window, just above, dances across the deadly surface, casting flickers into the darker corners at the far side of the room.

One of the smaller boys moves toward the basin, stands on tip-toe to gaze at the contents.

"You needn't bother, Pepper. They told us already, it's not safe to drink."

"It's poison," says one of the blonde-haired girls.

"Maybe they lied." Blue-eyed Franz shrugs as he speaks. "It wouldn't be the first time." He whispers the last sentence, as if in fear of being overheard.

The dark-eyed boy moves to the garbage pail beside the room's one door, opposite the window and bowl. While the others speculate over whether the water is truly poisonous or not, the dark-eyed boy finds something lovely. The core of an apple, eaten carefully down to the seeds and stem, but still full of sweet moisture. The boy sucks quietly on this treasure.

"Hey," calls Franz. "What's that you've got?" His voice attracts the attention of the others.

A scuffle breaks out as the remaining six boys, and two of the girls, fight first for the apple core and then for the right to search the garbage pail. But it is no use. The dark-eyed boy had already found the only source of wetness in the small bucket. Forgotten for the moment, he huddles silently in the darkest corner.

The others pant. The brief brawl has increased their awareness of thirst.

Fritz, to whom the others defer, speaks. "We need to know if the water is good to drink."

Several children lick cracked lips, nodding.

"Greta," he calls to a small shivering girl who had not participated in the struggle over the waste. "Come here and drink."

A visible shudder runs through her small body as she rises. She knows better than to resist Fritz. Her thick lashes, long and blonde, cover her eyes as she shuffles towards the basin.

The large boy arranges his features into what he believes to be a sincere and adult expression. "It is for the good of us all."

"Not all," whispers the dark-eyed boy in his corner. But no one hears him.

"No!" The cry is anguished, wrenched from a parched throat. A blue-eyed boy walks swiftly to block Greta's progress. "No, Greti," Gunther says. His eyes plead with her. "I'll try it," he says, running his small hand along the side of her face. His voice sounds brave, but he looks terrified as he dips shaking hands into the basin and drinks.

Nothing happens immediately. The boy joins hands with the

girl for whom he's been willing to brave poison. But within seconds, his frame seizes and shudders, and his blue eyes roll back in his head.

It takes him a long time to die. Greta holds his hand, singing to his tortured body until her voice leaves her. She does not cry; her body cannot form tears in its dehydrated state.

Three more children, driven mad by thirst, try the water in the darkness of the cold, dry night. In the morning, four small bodies are exchanged for a large barrel of good water and the children drink until they are sated.

n.b.: I suspected several would be unable to exert sufficient self-control in the face of the tempting water. The loss of Gunther exasperates me. The boy was clever. Still, it is better to be rid of a tender-hearted child now than to have a tender-hearted adult serving me in the future.

This test has revealed much. I will certainly administer it to the other litter.

-translation by G. Pfeffer

15

BIRTHDAY

A week passed and my birthday arrived. Things had been strange between Will and me. I wasn't the most experienced person when it came to boys and kissing, but it felt a little odd to me that Will didn't so much as hold my hand after telling me how he felt. The more I thought about it, the more confused I became about what exactly he had told me. Sure, the kiss said *I want you.* And that look in his eyes, like nothing this world had to offer compared to me, said *I love you.* But he hadn't put it into words, had he?

Sitting alone in the kitchen, I wished for the millionth time that I could ask Gwyn's advice. She'd be able to tell me what to do. What it meant if a guy wanted to spend every free moment with you but wouldn't kiss you a second time.

Gwyn. I sighed. I'd made the decision to live without her friendship. I was going to have to figure this out without her.

I thought again of Will's parting that evening after we'd kissed. His words had been all about staying friends.

Just friends.

Was that what Will *really* wanted? Maybe he was just trying out kissing me, kind of like trying out a new brand of running shoes, and he decided I wasn't his brand after all. *Ouch.* The thought stung. My eyes burned and then blurred with tears.

So what did I want? I wanted Will. I loved him; I felt sure of it. But what earthly good would it do me to tell him that I loved him if he'd already decided he didn't actually feel that way about me? If I was *Nike* and he liked *Brooks* after all?

I wanted Will in my life. I wanted it bad enough that I wasn't going to risk scaring him off. He could be *Brooks*-boy and I'd be *Nike*-girl and everything would go back to where it used to be. Just friends. Will had to stay in my life, what with *rippling* and Sir Walter and all that mess. So did I want him to feel like he had to walk on tip-toe around me because he'd broken my heart? No. I didn't want that. I wouldn't let him know how I felt. I couldn't.

But I wished I felt *sure* I was reading him right. I could talk to Sylvia. She and Dad would be back from the bakery with my cake in half an hour. But no, if Syl had any hint that Will had broken my heart, her inner lioness would come out, hungry for blood. Wouldn't that make for a great birthday party? And I didn't think she'd understand, anyway. She'd tell me about other fish in the sea or something when I already knew there was only one fish I wanted.

That left Mickie to talk to.

Yeah, right. The thought actually brought a smile to my face. She'd read Will the riot act for kissing a girl he didn't love, and then she'd ask how he could even *think* of kissing when there were people who wanted all of us *dead*, for the love of Mike. No, I wasn't bringing Will's sister into this whatever-it-was.

I could do *just friends*. When I thought of the empty years, the years I'd walled off my heart from anyone, I felt grateful for *just friends*. I stared down at my running shoes, thinking of all the hours they'd logged with Will pounding the road beside me. A thought whispered across my mind, seductive.

If you became Brooks-girl instead, maybe he'd like you.

I swallowed hard. That was an idea. How badly did I want him to like me? What would I be willing to give up, set aside, change? Could I buy a few magazines at the grocery store check-out and take a survey and—

I smiled, shaking my head. I liked being me—the me I was now. In fact, the great thing about hanging with Will, or Mickie, for that matter, was that I could be completely *me*. For the first time in eight years, I knew who I was. No way was I giving that up.

I looked at my Nikes again. "I like you. I'm not swapping you out for Brooks. This conversation is officially closed." I reached down to retie one of the shoelaces that had worked its way loose.

And as I tightened my laces, I had an odd thought. Why did my clothes and shoes come with me when I rippled? Why didn't they remain behind? This called for an experiment.

I picked up our coffee pot, half-full. I rippled, and the coffee pot came with me. I rippled back and set the pot down. I walked to the pantry and picked up a bag of onions. Twenty-five pounds, the packaging said. The bag came with me. But then, when I tried placing my hand on just one onion on top of the pile, the bag didn't come with me—only the single onion rippled. I could "sense" the onion in my hand. I *let go* of the onion, and after I rippled back solid, the onion was *gone*.

Weird.

Good thing I hadn't tried that with the coffee pot. My parents without access to caffeine in the morning? Not pretty. I wondered how big of an item I could bring with me.

The largest thing in the room that I figured I could lift stood by the sliding glass door. I crossed to a potted fichus tree, squatted, and picked it up—barely—and rippled.

CRASH! I was gone, but the pot remained, having dropped to the floor. Crap. I rippled back looking at the dirt and cracked pottery. The tree remained upright, held in place by the pot, but now there were a few missing pieces. Leaves fluttered sadly down. Sylvia was going to kill me. I started giggling, imagining myself explaining this to my folks. And then I sobered up. Because I was going to have to explain it any minute.

The doorbell rang and I let Mickie and Will inside. Will carried a large, flat object wrapped in rice paper.

"Happy Birthday," said Mickie.

"Come on in. My folks ran off for the cake, but they'll be back any minute." I closed the door behind them and we crossed into the family room.

Will pointed to the fichus tree and dirt. "Problem?"

I explained what I'd done.

"You can't ripple with anything that weighs more than you do," Will said. "Or anything that's larger, dimension-wise."

I walked to the pantry for the broom and dustpan. "I've got to get this swept up before Sylvia and Dad get back."

"Your parents left you on your birthday?" asked Will.

I began brushing the soil into a pile. "They're getting my cake. From Las ABC."

"Is Gwyn coming, then?" Will asked brightly.

I shook my head.

Mickie cleared her throat. "Hey, Sam, about Gwyn—"

"It is what it is," I said, grabbing another onion from the pantry. I didn't want to discuss Gwyn with Mickie on my birthday. "Catch, Will," I said, tossing the onion to him. "I want you to try something. See what happens if you ripple away and drop the onion and come back solid."

"Is this going to make another mess?"

"Just try it."

He shrugged, onion in hand, and rippled. Two seconds later he rematerialized, minus the onion.

Mickie's eyebrows raised. "That could come in handy next time I need you to take out the trash."

"I never tried letting go of something before," Will said. "Can I try that again?"

"Children, let's leave Sylvia's supply of onions alone." Mickie shooed us away from the pantry. "Sam, any chance of an update on Pfeffer's black book?"

I nodded and ran upstairs, returning with the book. "I figured out some of it. But you've got to keep in mind I'm still guessing on a lot of the words. The sections are like scenes—that's how I think of them, like scenes in a movie." I flipped to the center of the book and removed my notes. "This one is about what happens when the food doesn't match with the number of kids. This boy named 'Pebre' is asking where are his bread and milk. A big girl called Helga says there's only eleven servings and Pebre asks again, where is his food? And a big boy called Hans tells Pebre not to do something—I'm not sure what—by the window when it's time to eat. Then a smaller boy tries to share his food but Hans isn't having any of it and threatens the small boy, Karl, if he tries to share. And Karl is crying."

I looked up, grimacing.

"This book's a laugh a minute, huh?" Mickie shook her head. "The whole thing makes no sense to me. Why write it down? You'd have to be a total sicko. Does the writer ever identify him or herself?"

I shook my head. "No. But there's something interesting about one of the names: Pebre. All the other kids have names like Karl, Hans, Helga and so on. German names. This one kid has a name that doesn't fit. And I tried to find a translation for "pebre" online and I kept getting recipes for spicy sauces with peppers, so I started thinking 'oh, what if it means "pepper?"' See?"

Will and Mickie stared at me.

"Pepper in German is 'Pfeffer.' What if the kid's name is a nickname meaning pepper? What if Dr. Pfeffer lived through this mess?"

"He's not old enough, Sam." Mickie said it gently.

"Uh, Mick, what if he *was* old enough?" Will asked. He looked at me and then back to his sister. "There's this theory Sam has that I think you should hear about."

Will explained my theory about extra-long lives,

which he'd apparently been keeping to himself, 'til now.

She approved the theory, but not my idea about Pfeffer. "None of this proves anything. But I'll admit I didn't know that his name meant 'pepper.'"

"One time when I complained about how it sucked living with you, he said he'd been raised in an orphanage," Will said to his sister.

I snorted with laughter.

"It would explain his obsession with sauerkraut and German beer, if he grew up in Germany," said Will.

"And we know Helmann was set to be tried for experiments he performed on children at the time he was researching Helmann's Disease." Mickie's frown deepened. "I don't know. It's all circumstantial."

We sat silently. I considered reading from the next section, but then I heard the doorbell ring. Why would Syl ring the bell?

My stomach squeezed and I hoped it was Gwyn, coming to wish me happy birthday. I walked to answer the door, leaving Mickie in contemplation of Pfeffer's national origin. Sylvia stood outside balancing a ginormous chocolate cake. I could see Dad fiddling with the canopy on the pickup.

"I was afraid I'd drop it if I tried the door handle," said Syl, smiling. She greeted Mickie and Will, apologized for running late, and turned back to me. "Bridget made it special for you, sweetie. She didn't have time to frost it 'til after the bakery closed. She says,

'Happy Birthday.'"

But Gwyn doesn't. I buried the thought for now and smiled as Sylvia placed a cake on the table and Dad came in from the garage. Once we were all seated at the table, Will passed me his gift. I gently removed the ribbon securing the paper around the large, flat object. It was a framed photograph that Will must have taken. "Illilouette Creek!" I whispered. "Will, you're an artist."

"Mickie got it framed. It's from both of us," said Will.

"Thank you both. I love it."

Mickie murmured, "We wanted you to keep *good* memories of that day."

I reached across the table and squeezed her hand.

Sylvia lit candles which I blew out with a wish involving Will kissing me again and Gwyn changing her mind about being friends with me. Then we plowed through seven layers of alternating dark, milk, and white chocolate smothered in dark chocolate ganache.

For the record, chocolate's a pretty decent antidote for unrequited love.

Fat and happy, we rolled ourselves away from the table and trundled down to a large flat area we kept cleared for fall burning. Safety-Dad held a hose at the ready and handed the fire extinguisher to me. This year's brush pile was huge; Will, Mickie, and I sat nearly twenty feet from my parents, on the opposite side of the brush pile.

As we settled on rickety lawn chairs pastured here for this event each year, Dad lit the fire. The flames jumped from cornstalks to twigs and yard debris, carving an erratic path across from Dad and Sylvia's side towards the side where I sat between Mickie and Will. Soon the flames were too tall for me to see across to my folks.

We scooted back from the intense heat, me with fire extinguisher in hand. "I don't actually remember how to use this thing."

"I know how," said Will. "I put out kitchen fires twice at my old school. Neither time was my fault," he added.

I smiled and heaved the red canister to him. I could imagine Will having a cool head in a panicked kitchen or any other threatening situation.

Will poked at the fire, sending sparks zinging outside the fire circle. The blaze crackled noisily; I was sure Sylvia and Dad wouldn't hear anything we said at the moment. "So, any more 'wedding invitations' in the mail lately?" It had been over a month since the last letter arrived.

"Nothing," said Mickie and Will together.

"Which makes me worry if he's still alive." Mickie's face, lit by firelight, plainly showed her fear that he wasn't. "He's so old."

"He said he'd been real busy," I replied.

The bonfire popped, sending sparks whirling up

into the black October sky like fiery snowflakes. Most of the brush had burned down, and a few gnarled manzanita branches blazed hot and strong in the center. The manzanita burned so bright that I found it hard to look in any other direction; everywhere else was so dark.

The branches resembled arms reaching to the heavens. Calming. The flame looked like fiery clothing adorning those limbs as it twisted and swayed. Hypnotic. In spite of the intensity with which the manzanita burned, the heat had died down a bit. My face no longer felt like it was getting sunburned and my back finally felt warm and cozy although it was cold outside. A branch in the center burned through and the whole pile collapsed inward a foot.

My vision shifted and I saw Will's hand touching mine as he took a fire extinguisher from me. Then the manzanita fire came back into focus. I noticed Will pulling his hand back, as if he'd touched me. He leaned in and whispered, "You're invisible, Sam."

I looked down; he was right. This was new. Apparently fire-gazing was as relaxing for me as looking at water. I should have caught the clue of my temperature changing. I needed to pay more attention to my body.

I looked across to Sylvia and Dad. Their heads leaned together, gazing at the stars. They hadn't seen me vanish. I rippled back, smiling at my skin-clad hands, at the control I had over the coming-back-part.

Mickie let out a sigh next to me. "That was stupid Sam, but they didn't see. You need to be more careful."

"I'm sorry; it was an accident."

Will spoke. "I reached out to where you were sitting and I thought, 'come back, come back, come back,' but it seemed like you weren't hearing me. So then I tried saying something out loud."

"I heard you say, 'You're invisible, Sam,' and I might have seen an image from your head—the fire extinguisher from earlier?" I left out the part about seeing our hands touching.

"I was remembering that," Will confirmed.

"Maybe this thing we do isn't so much mind-reading as, I don't know, maybe 'image-reading.' I've never actually 'heard' your voice—just seen images. I'm sure I didn't *hear* you say 'come back.'"

He nodded thoughtfully.

Mickie whispered, "What the hell are you guys talking about?"

"You didn't tell your sister?" I looked at Will, shocked.

Will shrugged and explained it to her. Mickie was silent for a moment. Then she leaned past me to Will and said, "If you ever—EVER—try to get in my head, you are *DEAD*."

"Like I'd want to."

"Yeah, well if I catch you air-conditioning my personal space, I'll know."

"Whatever."

I shifted uncomfortably in my lawn chair. "So I guess it's not only water that, er, blisses me." I didn't bring up that Will kissing me did the same thing.

Mickie's phone vibrated. She opened it and read the text message. "Aw, crap," she moaned. "I have to finish a project by ten tomorrow. I'm sorry Sam, we're going to have to take off."

"Man, your job sucks, Mick," said Will.

"My job puts food on your plate."

"It's okay; I'm kind of sleepy anyway." I felt like a playground monitor breaking up a pair of children.

Mick and Will thanked my folks, and the three of us walked back around the house to the sliding glass door. Will sprang ahead a few steps, like he wanted to open the door for us. Instead, he rippled through it, grinning from the far side.

"Show off," Mickie muttered darkly.

Will *did* pull the door open for us however, and Mickie and I entered the house conventionally.

"You see what I have to put up with?" Mickie mussed Will's hair.

"Hands off," Will said. "I am *not* your baby bro anymore."

"You'll *always* be my baby brother." Mickie smiled.

Will turned to me as we approached the front door. "You see what I have to put up with?"

16

THE FLASHLIGHT MAN

"Your uncle called," Sylvia said the next morning as I poured milk over my cereal. "He says, 'Happy Birthday,' and he needs your dad's help on one of the farms. I'm keeping your dad company on the drive, okay?" She looked worried that I might not take the news well.

"No problem." I smiled to reassure her.

"We'll be back in time for dinner, okay?"

"Sure. I'll get in a good run." It had been awhile since any of the berry farms in the valley had called my dad away on a Sunday, but I had enough farmer's kid in me to know berries trumped weekends.

I waved as they drove off, and then I headed upstairs to put on my running gear. I thought about calling Will but decided what I really needed was some time to myself.

Out on the road, I took in cold gulps of October morning air. Without admitting it to myself, I knew where I was heading. I turned off the highway and onto Main Street, keeping my eyes fixed ahead as I ran past Las ABC, as if I didn't want to know whether it was Gwyn or her mom turning the lights on, flipping the sign from Closed to Open.

I slowed for an abbreviated cool-down, and passed the residential portion of Main Street at the far edge of town before turning into the tiny oasis of trimmed hedges and green lawns. No one else was here on a quiet Sunday morning, but then I usually had the cemetery to myself.

Four rows down, fifteen plots over.

I hunched beside my mother's grave and quietly spoke my thoughts to her. About losing Gwyn's friendship, about kissing Will, about turning sixteen, about how much I still missed her. My skin cooled and the breeze made my face sting where the tears left trails. I wished I'd brought a jacket. And then realized I had a solution to the problem of feeling cold.

I lifted one side of my mouth in a half-smile.

"Check out what I can do, Mom."

I relaxed into invisibility. And then I just sat, quiet and undetectable, beside the small grave marker of *Kathryn Elisabeth DuClos Ruiz, Beloved Wife and Mother.*

A man approached the cemetery. This was unusual.

Visitors usually turned aside rather than disturb the weeping girl whose story they knew all too well.

Oh. He couldn't see me.

As he approached my mother's resting place, I scowled, irritated by his presence. He peered through me at the words on the stone, muttering the date to himself and nodding. He looked around as if to see who else might reside in the ground beside my dead mother. There was no one; Dad had purchased the nearby plots. The man looked puzzled, even annoyed, as he took one last turn around my family's domain. He grunted and turned to go.

I watched as he strode towards Main Street. Who was he, and what the hell did he mean by coming to stare at Mom's grave? I rose, intending to run and catch up to him, but something funny happened when I tried running invisibly for the first time. I didn't think about the lack of resistance, about how rippling caused me to "glide" instead of moving normally. I reached the opposite end of Main before I realized how fast I could move in my friction-free state. I'd covered eight blocks in a matter of seconds! I knew I'd never done that before in a car, so I must have been running well over the twenty-five mile-an-hour speed limit. Weird, but not something I had time to think about at the moment.

I whirled back to face my quarry and saw him turning into Las ABC. Using a controlled stride this time, I followed the man as he pushed on the carved door of the café.

Gwyn looked up from texting behind the bakery case—her mom must not have been around—and welcomed the stranger. He ordered coffee and a slice of pie. Gwyn rang up the order, asking what brought him to Las Abuelitas.

"That obvious, is it?" he asked, smiling.

She shrugged. "I don't recognize you is all."

"I'm doing some research for the upcoming Sesquicentennial of the Yosemite Grant."

"Uh-huh," she responded, passing the pie slice across the counter. "What's the . . . whatever got to do with us?"

"The earliest European settlers here, the owners of the Las Abuelitas Rancho, were involved in the birth of the National Park. Exciting stuff for interpretive historians like myself."

"Hmmm." She poured his coffee.

"Would you mind if I asked you some questions about Las Abuelitas?"

"You can ask," she said, with a short giggle.

I smiled: she hated history even more than biology.

"I'll bet you know more than you think. Sit with me a minute?" He held out his hand, flashed a toothy smile. "Nat Wilke."

The café was empty. The guy had movie-star good looks. She shook hands and joined him.

"It looks to me like there are a couple of very old

buildings in town. What can you tell me about the cabin by the 'Welcome' sign? On the highway by the gas station?"

Will and Mickie's house.

I held my breath, figuratively speaking.

"It's old. You got that right." I saw a defensive wall come up; she wasn't willing to chat about Will and Mickie. "That's all I really know."

He nodded. "The next place down the highway is impressive. Is that a bed and breakfast inn? Innkeepers know more local history than anyone else, I find."

She snorted. "No, that's the Ruizes'. They're super-rich thanks to some fruit the dad invented."

"A farming family?" Nat Wilke nodded as he sipped coffee. "The joy of tilling the soil and seeing it yield forth. Farming must be the happiest of all professions and farmers the happiest of all men."

Gwyn looked at him with a "get real" expression.

"What? You disagree with me?" he asked, movie-star smile on his face. "I think the evidence is there: a mansion on the edge of a sleepy town. Wouldn't you call that lucky?" His face had this look, like hunger, almost, and I felt like I'd seen him before with that exact expression.

My invisible frame quivered.

"I think most farmers work pretty hard and don't have a big house to show for it at the end of the day," said Gwyn at last.

"Then *this* farmer is particularly fortunate."

Gwyn shrugged. I could tell she was losing interest in this guy with his nosiness and his attitude. "I've got work to do," she said, standing.

"I believe I saw a Ruiz grave. Cemeteries are as full of information as innkeepers." He flipped through a small notepad. "Ah, here it is: Kathryn Ruiz. Just the one grave; would that be the same farming family?"

He's digging for information.

Gwyn nodded, slowly wiping down an already clean table.

"I revise what I said about the farmer's luck," he said. "It appears she died young?" He inflected his voice just enough to try to force a response from Gwyn.

"She was pretty young," Gwyn agreed. "A drunk driver killed her and a little girl."

"A mother and her daughter killed by a drunk driver; that is a tragedy." He looked appropriately sorrowful.

Gwyn's eyes narrowed. She was deciding whether or not to correct his error. "I didn't say it was her daughter. You're not putting all this in your history-whatever, are you?"

His mouth pulled up into a smile on one side. The smile didn't extend to his cold, blue eyes. "Only what's relevant to the Sesquicentennial. But a healthy curiosity about the present often teases out truths from the past, I find."

"Well, I wouldn't go around town being all curious about the Ruizes. You'll find most people in Las Abs are pretty protective of them," said Gwyn.

"Of course," said the man. "I was being insensitive. A professional hazard for a historian, I'm afraid. Could I get the pie wrapped to go? I need to be in Oakhurst by 11:30."

"I'll get that boxed up right away," she said, her voice all business-like.

The man strolled beside the bakery case. "And I'll avoid asking questions about the unfortunate farmer, shall I?" He smiled his big Hollywood grin again.

Gwyn softened. "Yeah, well, small towns are . . . different. I lived in L.A. for seven years."

"So," said the man, leaning forward against the bakery case. I thought I saw a flash of something like eagerness in his expression. "Just between us, then, there was perhaps a child who lived? Someone to put some joy back into that poor farmer's life?"

"Yeah, something like that." She finished boxing the pie. "There's a daughter."

Nat took the pie from Gwyn, white teeth gleaming. "Thanks so much for your help."

"Come see us again," she replied.

What is it about you? I racked my brain. He must look like someone famous. Gwyn or her mom would know who. I followed him outside: the viscous glass of the old door embraced and released me.

Nat Wilke marched decisively down Main. Passing a trash can a block down from Las ABC, he chucked the pie in the receptacle. Okay, this guy did *not* go into the café for snacks. He wanted information. *Why?*

Standing in the middle of Main Street, he waited for an oncoming car to pass. He threw a quick glance over his shoulder and I knew: I knew where I'd seen him.

He was the *flashlight* man.

I suppressed a mental shudder. Moments after I'd seen Mom and Maggie run down, I'd thought I'd seen someone, a man, hovering over their bodies in the middle of the street. He was there and then gone, like when someone turns a flashlight on and off. I'd thought maybe he was an angel who had come for Mom and Maggie. Dressed all in white, he'd turned his face into the streetlight so that it seemed to glow before he disappeared.

But this was no angel; he was flesh and blood.

Who was he? I needed to know.

Syl and Dad would be gone another six hours easy. I made a decision. As Nat Wilke hit the key clicker to his sports car, I passed invisibly into the back seat.

He took the wrong turn as he left town, punching buttons on his cell phone. He wouldn't make Oakhurst by 11:30 unless he turned around soon. I listened as he left a message in perfect French: *The daughter lived.*

He'd been asking about *me*. And if I lived.

Nat took the straight stretch of road nearly forty

miles above the speed limit, but he slowed for the first big curve as we headed towards Mariposa. A half-dozen neatly stacked books slid through me upon the back seat of the vehicle. I glanced down and realized these looked exactly like the volume Mickie had given me. Except that all of these had been marked with sticky-notes. Some had a rainbow of stickies, some only a few. I saw the name *Elisabeth* on a couple of the notes, spelled like my mom's middle name, with an "s" instead of a "z." Another chill ran through me.

Who are you? I thought, staring at the man driving.

We slowed through Bootjack. Nat Wilke had apparently lied about going to Oakhurst. He drove like he knew where he was headed, but not like someone who truly knew the roads. He'd zoomed right through two speed-traps that locals slowed down for.

I began to calculate in my mind how far I could go with flashlight-man before I'd need to exit the vehicle and start back home. Of course, I'd just learned I could run faster than cars could lawfully drive through Las Abs. I figured that wherever we were at 3:30, I would leave him and retrace the journey back home.

We continued through Mariposa, and I started to think that coming with him had been a stupid idea. What did I think I would learn riding in a car with this stranger? He could be driving to San Francisco. Or Seattle. We passed a sign that said Merced was in forty-three miles.

"Eine halbe Stunde," he murmured.

German for "a half hour." We were heading to Merced. Sure enough, Nat Wilke pulled into the UC Merced campus, sleepy on a Sunday afternoon, and parked before an impressive building. I followed him, one last curious glance at the pile of black books.

The man card-swiped himself through several doors before stepping into an administrative office, deserted for the weekend. He ran his fingers along a row of mailboxes and located the one he wanted. It read *Dr. Gottlieb.* Had he been lying about his name or was he stealing someone's mail? The letters were addressed to *Dr. Helga Gottlieb.* He flipped through the stack, removing one and sliding his finger under the envelope flap.

"Scheisse!" He cursed his paper cut, speaking German again. He grabbed a handkerchief but evidently decided he needed something more permanent and opened several desk drawers muttering, "Band-Aids, Band-Aids."

I looked at the scattered envelopes. Crossed out on one of them, I saw the following: *Herr Dr. Pfeffer.* The envelope had been redirected in big loopy handwriting to Dr. Gottlieb.

Dr. Pfeffer? I wanted that letter.

Flashlight-man crossed to an adjoining room and rummaged for a first aid kit. Before I recognized what I was doing, I had rippled solid, grabbed the letter for Dr.

Pfeffer, and walked with it out into the hallway. I had a vague idea of how to exit the building and hoped the doors wouldn't lock me *inside*. I heard Nat re-entering the office. If he stepped out, he would see me. My heart began pounding crazy-fast, and I knew I couldn't find the calm I needed to ripple at the moment. I turned a corner and then another, looking for a place to hide and chill. At the third corner, I hurtled into a pair of guys the size of linebackers.

"What are you doing in here?" asked the larger of the two. "Can I see some ID?"

I was dressed for running, so I had no ID on me. I decided to pretend I was a UCM student. Fiddling with the letter in my hand, I spluttered out the first thing I could think of.

"I'm looking for Dr. Gottlieb's office," I said, glancing at the letter I held. "My, er, roommate got her mail by mistake. My roommate, Dee." I felt sweat gathering under my arms.

"Let's take her to Dr. Gottlieb." The taller one grabbed my arm above the elbow.

"Er, that's okay. You can give it to her." I held up my hard-won letter, hand shaking.

The two men surrounded me, and the shorter one grabbed my other arm. "This is a secured facility," he said. "How 'bout you explain to Dr. Gottlieb what you're doing inside of it?"

The two men were security guards, not football

players. The rings across their knuckles looked evil; how could I have mistaken them for athlete's rings?

We entered a room filled with scientific instruments and computers. And a woman with white-blonde hair.

"Dr. Gottlieb?" The man beside me spoke respectfully.

She looked up from a computer screen, clearly annoyed at the disturbance.

"This student was wandering the halls. She got past three security checks and claims she's here to see you."

"Who are you?" Her voice came out whisper-soft.

"Er, I'm Dee Gottlieb's roommate," I said. I held out the letter. "She got this by mistake. I think it's yours. You have the same last name."

Dr. Gottlieb took the letter but didn't move her eyes from my face. "You don't have a name of your own?"

The larger security guard squeezed hard on my arm. I winced.

"Who are you?" asked Dr. Gottlieb.

Her soft voice terrified me. Security-man gripped down again.

"Jane," I choked out. "Smith. I'm Jane Smith."

"Well, *Jane Smith*, how did you get into my lab?"

I lied wildly. "The doors weren't locked."

"Loosen her tongue, Ivanovich." Dr. Gottlieb tilted her head towards the shorter guard.

The blow came as an utter shock. I collapsed onto

the floor, one side of my face exploding with pain. It felt like my jawbone had been smashed through the roof of my mouth. I reached towards my face, my hand shaking so badly I missed and grabbed only air. A part of me expected the men and the woman standing over me to recoil in horror at this terrible accident. Like they couldn't have meant it to happen.

I took a breath to rise, but the room spun crazily with me at its center. And somehow my mouth had filled with something salty, metallic. The liquid tickled against my windpipe, and I coughed, spraying red from my mouth. *Blood.* I had a numb spot inside my cheek which was regaining sensation; I must have bitten down hard. I spat and spat, trying to rid my mouth of the flavor.

Helga Gottlieb smiled.

Ivanovich reached a hand down for me, my blood on his knuckles. I pulled back, but he forced me to stand.

"Are you certain your name is, ah, *Jane Smith?*" Helga asked quietly.

From the periphery of my vision, I saw the guard pull back as if to punch his ring-clad knuckles into my face again.

I swallowed hard and whispered, "Yes." Locking eyes with Helga, I braced, waiting for the man to strike. The hand around my arm tightened, but the blow didn't come.

"We'll just check your story, shall we?" Helga pulled up the corners of her mouth. It didn't look like a smile.

She strode to a door and pressed on a thumb-pad. The door unlocked silently and remained open. "Ivanovich, Jameson, seat her in there." She pointed inside the closet-sized room. "I'll look up student records for *Jane Smith*."

The guards pulled me into the small dark room. While one held my struggling form, the other swiftly and efficiently locked my ankles and arms into restraints attached to something that reminded me at first of a recliner. Then I realized it was actually more like the chairs at my dentist's office.

Sweat pooled under my arms, locked into place beside me. My heart, already beating fast, increased its pace and I felt an icy-prickling sensation in the pit of my stomach. I gazed down, hoping that somehow my mid-section had begun to ripple, but I was solid. The cold stabbing feeling in my belly had nothing to do with invisibility.

What would they do to me when they discovered I'd lied about my identity?

I felt beads of perspiration forming above my lips, along my hairline. With each intake of breath, I caught a rank odor rolling off of me. *This is what fear smells like.* The bleeding in my mouth had almost stopped, but the scent of my sweat combined with the metallic blood-smell turned my stomach. No way could I ripple in this state. Although I wouldn't want to ripple in front of people like this in any case.

Helga returned. Her thugs drew themselves to attention.

"Jameson," she murmured, "return to your duties patrolling the halls. Advise me at once if you find anyone else lurking about."

Helga stared at me; although her lips turned upwards, her eyes did not smile. The frosty orbs of palest blue unnerved me further, but I felt a flickering of resistance warming the ice-cold band around my stomach.

"You've lied to me, girl. I intend to discover the truth. I will ask you questions. Every time you choose to withhold the truth, Ivanovich will remove one of your teeth. We'll start in back to give you a chance to keep that pretty smile, shall we?" Again, she flashed her teeth at me. It was the feral grin of an animal hungry to kill and devour. "This procedure is normally performed with a painkiller, of course, but I believe we'll dispense with needles. For the present."

I tasted bile. Vomiting sounded like a good option at the moment; it might slow things down. But of course once I *wanted* to throw up, I couldn't. Moisture tickled its way from my armpits down across my sides and back. My hand flicked automatically to brush at the wet irritant causing the restraint to bite into my wrist. I realized something important. These cuffs were intended for someone with a larger frame than a running-addicted teen. I felt a flutter of hope that I could free my hands.

"Tell me your name." Helga's voice shattered the hopeful feeling.

Ivanovich picked up a sinister-looking instrument. *Pliers,* whispered some part of my brain. I opened my mouth to lie and realized I was screaming. Ivanovich's thick fingers, rough like sand paper, grasped my face and dug into the exquisite core of pain that was my jaw. He gripped harder, attempting to clamp the tool around a back molar. Trying to turn away increased the pain, so I stopped, tears streaming down my face as I squeezed my eyes tight shut. *There'll be lots more blood,* I thought.

Then Ivanovich removed his hand abruptly, and I opened my eyes to see that the man I knew as Nat Wilke entering the room.

"Ah, Helga. Always such a pleasure to see you hard at work." His tone was calm.

She seemed pleased to see him, murmuring, "Lieber Hansi," and running her hand affectionately across his face. He smiled pleasantly at her and then turned to stare at me with curiosity.

"Hans, you can assist me." Helga smiled at the flashlight man.

I felt the nausea returning along with the stabbing cold in my belly. Saliva formed in my mouth at an insane rate. *In a minute I'll drown in my own drool.*

Helga spoke again. "Ivanovich? Check that the security system is functioning properly and then rejoin Jameson." My tormentor dipped his head and left the room. I followed him with my eyes towards the outer door. He didn't use a card-swipe to leave.

Nat or *Hans*, whoever he was, touched a finger just below my right eye. Although his hands were softer than Ivanovich's, his touch lighter, I flinched.

He pressed cruelly, smiling, and then withdrew the finger. "And who is this?"

I shuddered. His nonchalance was even more frightening than the animal-like ferocity of the woman.

"*Jane Smith*, she says," replied Dr. Gottlieb. "I haven't yet determined her true identity."

"I don't suppose you have any identification hidden in that, er, running outfit?" asked the man.

I stared at him, remembering suddenly where I'd seen the names "Hans" and "Helga" paired before: the cruel children from the black book *scenarios*. Were these cold adults their descendents? My legs began to shake violently.

"I hadn't thought to remove her clothing," admitted Dr. Gottlieb. "She certainly used something to get past my card-swipe system."

"Yes, well, best to be thorough," the man said, nodding thoughtfully. Then he turned his full attention to Dr. Gottlieb. "I'm relieved to find you here. I *really* must speak with you. In private."

"Help me finish up with the student. Then we can talk."

"I would love to, but Father is expecting me to report back to him, and you know how tight a schedule he keeps."

"Phhht." She looked annoyed and anxious at the same time. "Of course. My private office, then." They crossed out of my sight and I heard a door open and close.

My heart pounding, I pulled hard at my wrists. The cuffs bit into my hand, scraping my knuckles, but both hands came free. I exhaled and reached down over my legs to yank off my running shoes in case I could wriggle my feet free. My legs felt jittery, but with excitement, not fear. Cautiously, I pointed my toes like a dancer and slipped one foot and then the other through the cylindrical shackles. Tucking my shoes under one arm, I eased myself off the seat, now slick with my sweat.

Hans and Helga remained behind her solid office door; they couldn't see me. Launching myself towards the door of the main room, I tried to do like Coach always said and channel my nervous energy into *speed*. Silently, I opened the door into the hallway. I eased it shut, cringing as it squeaked and clicked, and then I started down the hall searching for a bathroom to hide in and calm myself enough so I could ripple. This time I snuck a look before turning any corners. Around the second corner, I located a ladies' room and let myself inside.

The door closed, leaving me in darkness, safe and alone. I had way more questions than answers at this point, but of one thing I felt certain. I would *not* be hanging out here for Dr. Evil to strip-search me or finger-print me or pull out my teeth. I took several slow breaths to calm myself down.

As my eyes adjusted, I realized I could see enough from the exit-sign lighting to make out a sink. *Water!* I felt hope increasing. Slipping my running shoes back on, I then crossed to the water source and turned it on, letting the soothing sound relax me. I eased an injured hand into the stream of water. I thought of Will. Of his lips inching towards mine, of the bliss of the moment I'd thought he loved me. But then reality intruded; Will wanted friendship. *Just friends.*

I returned my focus to the steady rush of water, clear, lovely water, until I realized I couldn't feel the *wetness* or temperature or anything else. I looked down for my hands and found they were gone. So was all the pain I'd been feeling. *Bonus!*

I passed invisibly through the screech of the bathroom wall—cinder block—and into the lighted hallway. My eyes didn't need to adjust, I noted. *Of course not. You don't have eyes at the moment.* The thought made me smile. Well, think of smiling anyway. At both ends of the long hall, I saw signs indicating exits. While I considered which to try, I heard the voices of Hans and Helga once more. I stood to one side as they strode past me, speaking together about journals.

"I shouldn't have left them in the car," Hans said.

"My brother does have careless moments, after all," Helga said.

Brother? I followed them.

She continued. "Father will forgive you anything, you know. He'll probably say it was divine intervention that kept the girl alive."

"Perhaps he's right, in a manner of speaking. Her genetic material is invaluable."

"No more than mine," she said, sulky.

"Father does not see it that way."

"He risks a great deal, letting her live. I can dispose of her anytime, you know. I am so much closer in location than the rest of you."

"No!" Her brother's voice sounded angry and harsh. "Don't even jest about it. You survived your last action of this sort only because I pleaded for you myself. I persuaded him you saw the error of your ways, Helga."

"There was no error. I did what you were all too afraid to do. I did what needed to be done!"

"Your actions have raised public awareness of the disease at a time when Father wishes to suppress this awareness." He spoke calmly, as though to a child.

"We need to suppress the *gene,* Hans, not the public's knowledge of it."

"Father now questions the wisdom of eliminating all carriers of the chameleon gene. Fritz advises him that the genetic advances we had hoped to have in place by now are still a decade away. He will be very glad to learn that the daughter of Elisabeth's line has survived after all."

"I say our father doesn't know what's in his own best interest," said Helga. She lowered her voice, smiling. "You know I am right, Hansi. I could do it and make it look like an accident. No one but you would ever know."

"No!" he said sharply. "He's forgiven your other murders, but you wouldn't survive killing her. Do I have your word you will not harm her?"

Helga glared and then sighed. "You have my word."

The siblings approached the car.

"If there is an *accident,* I will not forget our conversation." Hans stared at his sister. "Do you understand?"

"You think he is right about her value?" she asked.

Her brother nodded.

"And he would truly kill me?" she asked quietly.

He spoke gravely. "We leave the girl until such time as Father is ready to act."

"Phhht. That could be decades."

The man shrugged. "Years, decades, it is not your concern. Or mine."

"Very well." Helga didn't look pleased as she agreed.

The man unlocked his car and retrieved the black books from the back seat. Helga took them carefully.

He stared at her, his head tipped to one side. "As for the intruder in your laboratory—nothing messy, sister dear. Be discreet. Pin the blame on one of your thugs. Allow one of them to defile her; it will look more convincing. Then kill him afterwards. Nothing flashy."

Helga smirked, not meeting her brother's eye.

"Your position here is no laughing matter. Do nothing further to draw Father's wrath. He is still very angry with you for causing such an uproar last August. We were flooded with media attention."

"He's forgotten I exist. I'll go mad if he leaves me here longer. Hans, you must convince him to forgive me and let me return to headquarters."

"He will forgive you—as long as you do nothing more to upset him. I'll speak up for you when I'm sure he's in a good mood."

"He'll be in a very good mood today. When you admit to him that you ran over the wrong girl nine years ago. You do admit I was right? You will tell Father that I was the one who said that *Samantha* survived?"

Me! The thought ricocheted through my brain.

The man gave a single quick nod.

"Ha!" she said. "I was right!"

"And I will listen to you more carefully in the future because you were right. But now you must listen to me. *Do not harm* this descendent of Elisabeth."

Helga frowned as Hans climbed in the car and drove away.

Did they mean Kathryn Elisabeth? Who were these two: *Helga and Hans*?

Could they be the actual children from the black book?

Hans and Helga.

They looked too young. Or did they? What if they had Rippler's Syndrome: then, could they be the same Hans and Helga?

The idea terrified me.

What do you know for sure? I asked myself.

The angel from my childhood memory had vanished before my eyes, like a rippler might do. And whatever Hans might be, he had definitely not been an angel come to gather Mom and Maggie's souls. It hadn't been drunken Harold who killed my mother and best friend: it had been murder. It had been Helga's brother: Hans.

The truth seared through me, more painful than anything I'd received in Dr. Gottlieb's laboratory. Instinctively, I found myself running down the road as I fled this new reality.

My mother was murdered. My best friend was killed in my

place.

These truths tasted like something bitter in my mouth, something I couldn't spit out or swallow away. My legs carried me down the road and I did the only thing my body knew how to do.

I ran.

I needed a long run, and I had one ahead of me. But the crazy-fast glide of running invisibly didn't feel right. I slowed myself along the long, flat stretch out of Merced and beyond Planada. Cars flew past me at a regular speed again. Familiar. Comforting.

My brain retrieved images from childhood. Maggie. Mom. Blood-marked asphalt. Things I didn't want to remember. I tried to refocus on my surroundings. A last pistachio orchard flew past and I reached the grassy-brown beginnings of the foothills. I ghosted past the rows of up-ended slate, tousled to earth's surface in some primeval earthquake. Leaning at drunken angles and covered with red lichen, they resembled blood-smeared tombstones. Something shiver-y ran through my invisible form; I could focus on the outside world all I wanted, but death grinned at me there as well.

Running slowly wasn't soothing me, but I wasn't ready to solidify and try conventional running. Ahead, the road twisted and cars slowed. I tried one last distraction: how fast could I move? I passed a mini-van on a hairpin curve. I set my sights on a BMW driving way too fast and found myself flying past. A sense of calm grew inside me as I focused on passing every car, every truck. I had no idea how fast I was going, but it felt right. I felt like Sam again.

Like Sam.

But who was I? Who was Samantha Ruiz, daughter of Kathryn Elisabeth? Why was I important to Helga and Hans's father, and who was he? Would Mickie know? Helga was getting Dr. Pfeffer's mail now—that was an important connection, surely.

I knew this much: I wasn't the same girl I'd been at the beginning of the day. I'd followed *the flashlight man* for one simple reason: because I wanted to know the truth.

Well, I knew it now.

Hans and Helga's *Father* had wanted me dead once. That was bad. Now he wanted me alive. Was that better or worse?

As I flew along the narrow highway back to my home, I knew this much: never again would I be a passive observer of my own life. Today changed everything. I would figure out the connection between Pfeffer and the black book and Hans and Helga and my mother's death.

I reveled in my speed, laughing to myself. *Catch me now!* I thought. Then I sobered, recalling how I'd been unable to calm enough to ripple back at the lab.

That couldn't happen again.

I would learn to control this ability and use it

whenever and under whatever circumstances I might need in the future: for the day when Hans and Helga's father "chose to act," whatever that meant.

And Will would help me.

A rush of warmth and gratitude flooded through me.

Gathering the thought of my friend tight to myself, I pulled down the stretch of road leading to my home.

17

CONFESSION

I showered fast, not even taking the time to apply cover-up to the ugly bruise on my cheek; the cut I ignored as well. It could wait. I threw on a fresh pair of sweats and my running shoes to run to Will's. I could have driven, but I knew that running would help me feel strong enough to do what I needed to do.

I needed to tell Mickie and Will what I'd just learned. But as I ran, a fresh thought overtook me.

This new information could drive Will out of my life forever. Whatever Mickie made of it, how could she fail to see this as a threat to Will's safety, and to her own?

Tears pricked the back of my eyes. *It's not fair!*

If I didn't tell them, Will would stay and life would continue as normal. That was all I wanted: for things to be normal.

But nothing could be normal for me ever again. And hiding the truth from Will and Mickie could prove deadly. Hans and Helga's father might want *me* alive, but how would he feel about Dr. Pfeffer's former assistant?

Either Hans or Helga could have participated in Pfeffer's death. Hiding what I knew? It could be a death sentence for Will and Mickie.

Telling what I knew?

I couldn't breathe. How could I live without Will?

I pulled off to the side of the road, stuck between nausea and tears, and crumpled to the ground, digging my fingers into the cold, dry dust. My breath came in short starts as the sobbing began. I let the day wash through me, tears stinging the cuts on my face, a chill wind gusting past. The crying came as a relief; I didn't think, didn't plan, just grieved. And then the time for crying passed, and I knew what I had to do.

I rose and turned to the Baker's cabin. No more hiding from the truth, no matter how dark. If I loved Will, I had to let him know. If he wanted to leave, I had to let him go.

I pounded on the door.

"Sam?" Mickie greeted me like I was an extra phonebook that just showed up on the front porch.

Will called from the kitchen sink, his back to me. "What's going on? Need help polishing off your birthday cake?"

"Um, no," I said. "Can I come in?"

"Of course," said Mickie, as she reached to open the door wider. "Sorry, Sam, I had to get up way too early. I'm not at my best today."

"You don't have a best," said Will, drying his hands on a worn towel.

"Shut up," replied his sister. "Let Sam talk."

"Oh, man! What happened to your face?" Will looked at my bruises and the tiny cut along my cheek. "You lose a fight with the road?"

"Not exactly," I said. I took an extra deep breath and started talking before I had time to change my mind. "Um, okay. So I want to know, what would you do if you found out that the researcher in Pfeffer's old lab had been party to the deaths of my mom and Maggie?"

"Come again?" said Will.

"What are you talking about?" asked Mickie.

I described encountering the "flashlight man" and how I'd hitched a ride to U.C. Merced. I smoothed some of the details about Helga's blood-thirsty games, but I had to admit my story sounded bad even without those details.

Mickie got quiet and let Will ask all the questions before I had even gotten to the part where they strapped me down. I hoped it was a good sign that she wasn't walking around packing things into boxes.

"Let me see if I got this straight," said Will.

"Pfeffer's replacement at the University has a brother who tried to kill you, Sam, and knows that you're alive after all, and this same dude has a Dad who wants your genes?"

I nodded. Mick's face looked paler than I'd ever seen it. I started wishing she'd do something, even haul out the boxes, instead of just sitting there with no expression on her face, staring out the back window.

We were all silent for a couple of minutes.

"Pfeffer said Las Abuelitas was safe," whispered Mickie, at last.

"No, Mick, he said to *try* Las Abs. He didn't say what we should try it for. He never said it was safe here," said Will.

"I'm not going to argue the point with you. Pfeffer meant for us to live here," said Mickie. "That's why he paid our rent. Why would he send us somewhere that wasn't safe?"

Will shrugged. "Maybe he meant for us to find Sam here. Maybe he knew about her."

"Okay, I don't even want to think about the implications of what you just said." Mickie shook her head slowly. "Everything I've done to keep Will safe . . ."

I'd seen Mickie angry before. I knew Will considered her volatility humorous at times. But this wasn't funny. She had a look I'd seen before at the zoo, the look of a caged animal desperate to escape.

"I'm taking Sam home," said Will to his distressed sister. He looked at the cut on my face again. "And you need to get that looked at."

"No!" said Mickie. She pulled one hand through her hair like she wanted to tear it all out. "No, Sam, no doctors. No records. Whoever's down there at UCM still thinks you were just some random student, but the first place they'll check to discover your true identity will be urgent care facilities, emergency rooms."

Her logic was impressive, especially considering she looked half-crazed at the moment.

"You *are* sure they didn't guess your true identity?" asked Mickie.

"I'm sure," I said. "I told them I was a student. They believed that, at least."

Mickie came closer, looking at the injuries on my face. "A butterfly bandage," she murmured, turning to rummage through a kitchen drawer. She carefully applied ointment and an odd-shaped bandage to the gash on my cheek.

I winced but held still.

"Leave that on for the next week," said Mickie.

I nodded.

"Come on," said Will. "I'm getting you home."

"Okay," I said. "Bye, Mickie. I'm sorry for all this."

"What?" she asked. "No, no it's not your fault. Better to know where we stand. Much better. You can't protect yourself from the enemy you don't know exists."

She crossed to her computer and began muttering and typing, seeming to forget me.

"Let's go," said Will.

I followed him out to his sister's Jeep.

"What will you do?" I asked, miserable.

Will shook his head. "Don't honestly know."

My heart sank. I tried to speak, but the words caught as my throat constricted. I blinked back tears.

"Hey, you know my sister. She's all smoke and steam. She'll get used to the idea."

I forced myself to talk as we drove down the highway. "What if she doesn't? What if she wants you to move?"

"I'll just say no." Will laughed, but it sounded hollow, like he was trying to convince me of something he wasn't sure of at all.

"What if she convinces you?"

Will down-shifted to bring the Jeep into my driveway. "We'll cross that bridge when it . . . does whatever bridges do. Geez, Sam, I don't know what to tell you. You know my sister. I just have to convince her that it's safe here."

"If you can," I said, my voice a whisper.

He smiled, reached over to touch the back of my hand, then pulled back like he changed his mind. "I'll be in touch, Sam."

He put the car into reverse, and I reached for the

door handle. He smiled at me, but the smile didn't quite reach his eyes. He looked a million miles away already and I wanted to reach over and grab him and not let go and tell him how I didn't think I could live without him even though I knew he just wanted to be friends and didn't that count for something and couldn't he pick me over his sister since I needed him more than she did?

But I just said, "Bye, then," and got out of the car.

A thin drizzle began. My feet felt like they weighed a hundred pounds each as I shuffled to my front door. Upon reaching it, I heard a squeal of brakes and turned to see my Dad slamming on the brakes to avoid hitting Will. I shuddered and ran inside to lick my wounds.

18

ACCIDENT

After telling Dad and Sylvia that I'd fallen while running, I climbed in bed and pulled the covers over my head. But then it got stuffy under my blankets and I worried I'd asphyxiate. I crawled out of bed and tried cleaning my room. Folding and hanging clothes proved too monotonous to shut my brain down. It whispered hateful things to me.

Will's leaving.

You saw how scared Mickie looked.

Will's gone.

How would I survive if that were true?

I found a favorite running sock—my good luck sock—in the back of my closet. It had been missing when our team ran our fun-meet. We lost, and it was my fault because I hadn't cleaned out my closet. The layers of things that were my fault started piling up.

Stop thinking about it, I said to myself, stuffing shirts into the laundry basket. But it didn't help. If I hadn't followed Hans today, none of us would be in panic mode right now. Mickie and Will wouldn't have a care in the world about living here. *If you weren't still alive, they'd be perfectly safe.* The thought hit me like an icy blast.

It was true.

I redoubled my efforts on my room, determined to drive the thoughts away. I snapped my sheets taut and plumped my pillows. I shook my duvet and settled it across the bed. The first tear hit as I began smoothing my duvet where it lumped at the bottom of the bed.

Stop crying!

I tugged at the comforter, smacking it to make it lie flat. But a bulgy lump remained and the tears came faster. I fell in a coiled heap at the foot of my bed, leaning my head upon the bed, my fist pounding at the bump under the covers.

Something jingled. I looked up and flipped back the duvet. Another jacket of Will's. With coins in the pocket—two dollars in quarters. I remembered the cold morning he'd loaned me this jacket, joking with me that those quarters better still be zipped inside or his running gear wasn't getting washed.

Because Will and Mick didn't live in a normal house with a mom and a dad and a washer and a dryer. And now, thanks to me, they'd be scared every day they remained in Las Abs. Closing my eyes tight, I tugged at Will's jacket and held it to my face, breathing in the smell of sweat and mown grass and some indefinable scent that was Will. And I cried 'til my eyes hurt.

An hour later, Sylvia tapped on my door letting me know dinner was ready. She stuck her head in, and I muttered something about my stomach feeling off and crawled into bed looking convincing enough that she felt my forehead, frowned and finally said to holler if I needed anything, closing the door behind her.

I need something, but you can't get it for me, I thought. I needed Will to call and tell me his sister had decided staying in town was as safe as any other option. I let another hour pass before I texted, knowing full well Mick might be the first one to see what I sent. I figured "How's it going?" was neutral enough.

I waited.

A minute passed.

Nothing.

Another minute. Ten.

Still nothing.

I flipped my phone on and saw a message about my text being undeliverable. I'd probably punched in the wrong number or something. I tried again, this time watching the screen for the "text message sent" indicator. Instead, the undeliverable message showed again. I tried a third time, my heart sinking, already knowing I'd see "undelivered" once more.

Why was their phone not working?

As I sat up, Will's jacket slid away and to the ground. I reached for it, as solid tangible proof that things were just fine, that a dead phone number meant nothing worse than . . . than what? I ran my arms inside the jacket, slid my feet into a pair of shoes and ran to my bathroom. I had to get back to Will and Mickie's.

It's okay, I said to myself as I turned on the faucet. I cleared my mind and centered all my thoughts upon the column of water flowing noiselessly into the basin. *Everything's going to turn out fine.* Turning off the overhead florescent, I tilted my head from side to side, which made the reflection of the plug-in night-light flicker through the smooth descent of water. It was beautiful. It made me think of the bonfire last night.

Last night, a million years ago; last night, when I'd been happy. I noticed a shimmer on the mirror telling me I'd rippled. Swiftly, I descended the stairs and passed outside through our front door. A woods-and-sand scent brushed through me, but I didn't have room in my mind for more than a single, burning thought.

Will can't be gone.

I ran the mile to their cabin so fast I passed a speeding Highway Patrol car.

The cabin was dark. The Jeep was missing. I dashed around back, my heart sinking, and discovered what I most feared: the pull-behind trailer, symbol of their vagrant existence, was gone.

256

No, my heart cried out. I crossed to the back door and passed inside. Tidy. Dark. Emptied of the few items Will and his sister had owned.

No, I whispered without a voice.

Will was gone.

***

I awoke the next morning to the sound of a man's voice, whispering soft and low.

"Sam? You awake? Sam?"

Will, I thought, struggling through the surface of sleep into day. I sat up, too fast, and my head spun. But even in the bare light of dawn, I could tell it wasn't Will.

"Dad?" I asked, voice rasping with thirst. "What time is it?"

"Sammy, I need you to be brave, honey," said my father.

I sat up. "What is it?" Had my dad heard about Will and Mickie's departure? I knew the rumor-mill ran twenty-four-seven in our small town.

"It's your friends, Sammy," said my dad. The compassion in his voice was touching. He *did* care about me, even though he'd been a jerk about the Bakers on more than one occasion.

"Yeah," I said, rolling away to face the wall. "They left." A lump in my throat told me the night's rest had restored my supply of tears.

"Honey, there's been an accident," said my dad.

There's been an accident.

Four very simple words.

Simple enough a child might say them. Simple enough they were the exact words I'd chosen when I called 9-1-1 as a child of seven. *There's been an accident.*

I don't remember getting to my feet, but I must have. My dad was holding me as I shook my head, screaming, *"No, no, no! You're wrong!"*

But I knew he was telling the truth. I'd awakened in the middle of the night, my heart pounding from an evil dream I couldn't remember, and as I'd slipped back into the darkness, I'd said a prayer for Will and Mickie, afraid in that quiet-of-the-night way that still haunts you in the morning.

"Mickie's beat up pretty bad, but Dr. Yang says she'll recover," said my dad.

I couldn't speak. I couldn't ask the next question.

"No one knows where her brother's body—where her brother is," said my dad, his voice cracking on the last word.

"They were together," I said, not like a question, just a flat fact.

"It's not clear right now, honey."

Dad drove us to Doctor Yang's home on the far side of Las Abuelitas.

"Why aren't we going to the hospital?" I asked.

"Mickie got a little hysterical about checking into

the hospital. She called for your step-mother, and Sylvia agreed that Mickie's wishes should be respected. There's something about not wanting their dad to be able to trace their whereabouts."

I nodded as Dad turned off the engine. "They don't want to be found," I agreed.

I ran to the door, desperate to talk to Mickie, to hear her tell me that my dad was wrong, that Will was fine. But when I got to the door, I couldn't bring myself to knock. What if Mickie couldn't tell me what I needed to hear? As I stood, anguished, outside in the cold morning air, Sylvia opened the door from inside and pulled me in with a warm hug.

"She wants to talk to you," said my step-mom. "In the dining room."

The Yangs' dining area had been turned into a small surgery room and Mick lay, covered in bandaging, upon what looked like a padded table.

"Hey," murmured Will's sister.

"Mick, I'm so sorry," I began, but how could I say out loud all the things I felt sorry about at the moment?

"Yeah, no worries," she said. "Sylvia, if you don't mind, I'd like to talk to Sam alone."

My step-mother smiled, squeezed my hand, and left, closing the solid-looking door behind her.

I wanted to speak. I wanted to ask a hundred questions or just one burning one. But I could only stare and blink back tears and wait for Mickie to say the words that would color the rest of my life.

She made a rumbling sound that I realized meant she was clearing her throat. "Have you seen him?"

This wasn't a question I expected. "Seen . . . Will, you mean?"

"Yes, Will. Have you seen my dumb-ass brother?"

Tears spilled out and down my face. She didn't know, then. And now it had become my job to explain to her that no one had recovered his body.

19

RECOVERY

"I'll kill him," said Mickie, before I could say anything. "I'll freaking kill him next time I see him. Then we'll see who gets the last word. Little brat." She took in a breath, slowly, like it hurt, and clutched at her side. "Idiot could have pushed me a little farther from the steering wheel while he was at it. Damn ribs are killing me even with whatever the doc pumped me full of."

I stared at her, trying to make some sense out of her ramblings. And then the words just tumbled out because I needed, on a cellular level, to know that Will was okay.

"Will's not dead?"

Mick laughed and then grunted, "Ow! Can't laugh—aye carumba!"

I thought my heart would stop beating while I waited for her to answer my question.

"No, the little bastard's not dead, as far as I know." She closed her eyes. "Although he's going to wish he was when I see him again."

"I don't understand," I said. "I thought . . . Dad said . . . I was afraid . . ." My voice shook with emotion, and Mick reached over to grab my hand.

"Will's fine," she murmured. "We had a falling out, and I packed the house, and he took off. I didn't know where he went. Didn't *want* to know. I just kept packing and got everything in the pull-behind, and then I didn't know what to do 'cause it's not like I wanted to leave a forwarding address sitting on the kitchen counter."

Mickie paused and took in a few slow breaths. "So then I'm just sitting there in an empty house trying to figure out what to do, and he rematerializes by the back door and starts arguing with me again about not moving. And finally he says he'll come along for the ride so he knows where I'm moving to, but he's coming along *invisible*, the little twit."

I could picture his face, dark eyes flashing with anger. My mouth tugged up on one side, but I hid the smile quickly for Mickie's sake.

"So I said fine, he could do whatever he damned well pleased and we took off. Well, I took off with my see-through brother presumably in the car on the highway to Fresno. And things were fine 'til some dumb-ass driver falls asleep at the wheel and crosses into my lane, and I suddenly have to choose between car crash or going off a cliff."

I gasped.

"Yeah, not much of a choice. Then Will comes solid and pushes me and steers the car and next thing I know there's emergency lights flashing from a response vehicle and I'm strapped on a gurney and they're asking for ID since the car tags and registration are smashed to bits."

"Oh, no," I murmured. "And Will?"

Mickie shrugged one shoulder, then grimaced from the motion. "He's around somewhere. He rippled again just before impact."

"How do you know?" I asked, my voice so quiet I worried she wouldn't hear it.

"He did this thing. When we were kids, he'd brush through me three times to let me know he was around and . . . safe. Because of Dad, you know."

I nodded.

"Icy cold. Always three times. He kept doing that on the ambulance ride. I finally said something 'cause I wasn't exactly enjoying the deep freeze treatment and then he stopped. Took off maybe."

Will was safe!

"Your step-mom really saved the day," said Mickie. "She barreled down the hill to find us, well, me, and she talked the EMT's into keeping the whole thing off-record. God only knows what that's going to cost."

"Money's not an issue," I said, hoping to reassure Mickie.

"Funny, that's what Sylvia said. But I owe her. Owe you guys. I'm sure she paid for the ambulance ride, whatever crap she gave me about it not costing anything. It's being billed and recorded somehow, somewhere, just minus my name. Not to mention this," she said, waving vaguely at the room full of medical equipment.

"Doctor Yang's a family friend," I said.

"Yeah, well, looks like I've got a whole family of folks who want me to stay put in the very place I don't want to be found."

I frowned. "I'm so sorry, Mickie. It's all my fault."

"Oh, please. Nothing here is your fault Sam. It's my idiot brother who started the whole thing being born with rippler's genes."

"I'm sorry," I began again.

"Sam, if you're trying to apologize for someone thinking they killed you and then finding out they didn't, I am not going to be answerable for my actions. Please don't tell me you think you are in any way to blame for this whole sorry mess."

Tears squeezed out of my eyes, closed now, as I tried to find some way to believe this wasn't my fault. But it was. Obviously. "You left town because of *me*. And you got in an accident," I whispered.

"Listen up, Sam. And listen good, 'cause each breath I take is kind of killing me at the moment." She paused to take another breath, wincing slightly. "I left because I *chose* to leave. Because I got scared of my own shadow. Because I was pissed at my brother. It's not your fault. None of it."

"But, the accident," I said.

"Oh, what? So now you're God and you orchestrated things so I'd end up on the other side of the road when some idiot fell asleep at the wheel? Sam, please. Wake up and read the bumper-stickers. Shit happens. Not your fault. You try apologizing one more time, and I swear I will get up and *walk* to Fresno so I don't have to listen to you being stupid anymore."

Through the tears streaming down my face, I smiled. Then I laughed. "Can't let that happen. Your brother would kill me."

"Yeah, well, he'd have to get through me first," said Mickie. Suddenly she looked exhausted. "Call the doc, will you? I want more whatever-it-is in my veins."

"Right away," I said, wiping my face with the back of one hand.

"Tissue by the gauze packs," said Mick, her words slurring.

I'd snotted my entire face and it took four tissues to dry off.

Outside, Sylvia and my dad looked anxious. "She's doing well," I said. "And her brother's safe."

"Safe?" asked my dad.

"She was saying things about Will being in the car with her," said Sylvia. "The EMTs said sometimes a body can end up . . . a long way from an accident. Some of your dad's friends who volunteer with search and rescue are out there now that it's light."

"They won't find him," I said. "Truly, he's safe."

My dad and Sylvia exchanged glances.

"Honey, you're sure?"

"I'm sure. He'd be here except Mick's really mad at him right now. They've . . . communicated." I felt my face flushing; I'm not good with deceit.

"I'll tell them to call off the man-hunt," said my dad, reaching for his cell.

"And she wants me here," I said. I felt sure of it, even though she hadn't made the request; I knew Mick wanted me with her. "So I'm skipping school today."

Dad was busy on the phone; Sylvia frowned, then said, "Okay, honey. Maybe that's for the best. Mickie thinks the world of you. She kept talking about you on the drive, and she made me call you as soon as Doctor Yang finished her stitches."

I smiled and things in the universe shifted a bit back into place. Then I felt puzzled. "Syl, why didn't you wake me up and take me down with you when she called?"

My step-mom sighed and her forehead wrinkled with worry. "Honey, it was a car accident. All I knew was that Mickie survived. I didn't know if . . ." She paused. "I thought you might . . ." She stopped again. "I didn't wake you because I was afraid of how scared you'd be. I couldn't send you to the site of an accident." Tears pooled in her eyes. "I'm sorry," she whispered.

And now it was my turn to tell her not to be sorry and that it was okay and that everything would be fine.

And a part of me believed it, even.

Dad and Sylvia decided I'd be okay on my own at the Yang's.

"Call if you need me, honey," said Syl.

"Call me," said my dad. "Your step-mom needs serious shut-eye."

I smiled. "I'll be fine. Go on." I shooed them out the front door and blinked back a few straggler tears, grateful for family.

Dr. Yang and his wife got ready to go to work, and Dr. Yang gave me his pager number "in case she needs anything before lunch," when he would return and check on his patient.

I walked back into the dining room and melted into one of the padded chairs. Mickie lay snoring lightly, looking utterly peaceful.

If only it could last.

20

FAMILY

I had fallen asleep, my head flopped to one side, and a man's voice, low and quiet, was speaking to me.

"Sam," he said.

"Dad?" I blinked my eyes open.

Will!

"Hey Sam," said Will. "I don't want to wake up my sister. You want to go into the other room with me?"

I rose and we left the dining room.

"You're okay?" I needed to hear it from him.

"As you can see." He smiled, full red lips sliding over white teeth. "At least until my sister wakes up. Something about how she's going to kill me the next time she sees me."

"Have you been here this whole time?" My

stomach squeezed. Did he see me crying when I thought he was lost?

"No, I took off once Dr. Yang started fixing up my sister."

"Where'd you go?"

"UC Merced," he said.

I gasped.

"I rippled. I wanted to find out a few things about who's using Pfeffer's old lab."

"Please tell me no one saw you," I said, squeezing my hands into tight fists.

"Relax," Will said. He looked at me and shook his head in a gesture of defeat. "How am I going to tell Mickie if *you* don't take it well?"

"I'm taking it well," I said. "This is me. Taking it well." I released my fisted hands. "See? No problem."

Will smiled and continued. "It was weird being back in Pfeffer's lab again. I mean, Mick used to practically live there. Well, until Pfeffer started getting all paranoid."

"Will, you do see now he had some good reasons to be cautious, right?"

"Yeah, sure. Don't get me wrong--I'm grateful for his paranoia. It's probably what saved our lives, even if it didn't save his."

"It must have been hard, being there again."

Will shrugged his shoulders. "Yeah. I miss Pfeffer, that's for sure. We could use his smarts. But here's the thing: he wanted us to come here. I'm more sure of it than ever. And I can't help thinking maybe it was so we could find you."

"Maybe," I said, my voice a bare whisper. I didn't trust myself to say more.

"That's what I think, anyways. And if he was so freaked about … risks, I think we're safe here. Safe as we are anywhere, I mean."

I wanted to believe it. Maybe it was true.

"I'm not changing my mind," said Will. "About staying. I've got to believe that someday, somehow, we'll figure everything out. Me and Mick. And you. I'll tell you one thing, though: I'd give anything to have Pfeffer back right now."

I nodded.

"I wonder if Sir Walter could help?"

"Yeah," replied Will "Me too."

"The French club trip is only six weeks away. I mean, if you're still going." I held my breath, waiting for his response.

"Of course I'm going, Sam." Will's eyes, large and dark, stared into mine. "I'm not moving from Las Abs no matter what my sister does." He grunted. "I don't think she believed I'd really stay here without her. Guess I didn't believe she'd leave without me, either."

"You're both idiotically stubborn," I said.

A low groan sounded from the dining room; Will and I jumped up.

"Get in here so I can kill you," said Mickie. "Don't protect him, Sam. I know he's in the house. I can smell the stink from here."

I laughed.

Will walked in ahead of me to his sister. Tenderly, he moved a stray curl off of her face.

"You've looked better," he said.

"You're still ugly," she retorted. "Where's Sam? I want both of you over here because I'm only going to say this once. And if you ask me about it later, I'll say it was the pain-meds talking."

I came up beside Will, smiling at his sister.

She took in a breath, wincing slightly. "I was wrong to try and leave. Sam, you're family. We're staying here until it's time to go to France."

I wanted to hug her. I wanted to hug Will. I hugged my arms around myself and grinned 'til my face hurt.

Mickie continued. "If we left now, our names would be on everyone's lips, and we don't want that. I saw it all clear as day when that car hit me. That accident should have been tonight's news. Thanks to Sylvia, that won't happen. But if Will and I disappeared, it would happen. This may not be the safest place on the planet for any of us, but I'm betting we'll be safer here for the next six weeks than we would be anywhere else with rumors flying around about how we left town."

271

"My sister *does* have a brain," murmured Will.

"I'll de-brain *you,* idiot," said Mickie. "Besides, we owe it to Sam. If Hans comes after you, Sam, I'll sick Will on him. I'm pretty sure Will's bite is septic."

Will chuckled quietly and took his sister's hand, giving it a quick squeeze.

"This is home," murmured Mick as her eyes drooped shut. "We're family."

I looked at Will and then at his sister. "Family," I agreed.

Will put his arm around my shoulder and steered me out of the Yang's dining room. "She needs sleep," he whispered, leaning in close so as not to wake his sister.

His breath felt warm in my ear, a small glowing heat I could carry inside me.

"You want to go outside for a minute?" I asked. "Catch the sunset?" The Yang's backyard overlooked the west. I didn't think they'd mind us hanging out there.

We strolled out and stood side by side, shoulders almost-but-not-quite touching. The evening was mild, unusual for late October. We stared out at the sunset, watching the last sheen of gold disappear into a purple haze over the San Joaquin Valley. I tilted my head up to stare at the sky overhead. It was grayish-bluish-purple.

"Knowing the truth about Mom's death . . ." I

paused, gazing at the vast heavens. "I'm glad I know now. There's . . . *purity* in knowing. Even if the truth is dark, there's still beauty in knowing it at last."

"Sham-Sundar," Will whispered the unfamiliar phrase.

I turned to look at his face, chiseled in the afterglow of the setting sun.

"What did you say?" I asked.

"A classmate from India told me his word for this time of evening, when it's between day and night. He called it 'Sham-Sundar.' Literally, it means something like 'the dark and the beautiful.'"

"Like the truth sometimes," I murmured. "Dark but beautiful."

"Like the truth sometimes," Will said, nodding. "What's that poem, the one they wrote on the Greek's Urn?"

I smiled, breathing out a soft laugh. "Not on it— about it. 'Ode on a Grecian Urn,'" I said. "Beauty is truth, truth beauty, —that is all ye know on earth, and all ye need to know."

"That's the one," said Will. "All you need to know."

I felt a rush of joy, that elusive emotion. If I closed my eyes, I could hear the flutter of a sheet from my childhood and see the lake spread out before me. But I didn't want to close my eyes; I didn't need to hide in the past anymore.

"First star," said Will, pointing overhead to the darkening canvas. "Make a wish."

I smiled at Will, and he smiled back, and in the warm reflection of his eyes I saw myself exactly where I wished to be.

THE END

For information on all releases by Cidney Swanson:
cidneyswanson.com

Acknowledgements

I'm bound to leave out someone important here, so I apologize in advance. I should have written these months ago when my brain wasn't fried from spending too many days in a row nit-picking my novel. But I didn't; so here goes.

Thanks to Deanna Stollar, the first person to provide a critique. Thanks to my Big Sur buddies Rhonda and Kristen who provided the most recent feedback. Neighbor and teacher Liz Engstrom: big hug! JMatt contributed planks along the bridge to publication. Maggie Stiefvater wasn't afraid to give it to me straight, the good and the bad. (Maggie, you define rock star.)

Katie, Rachael, Toby and Isabel: thanks for loving it from the first, and I'm sorry you (along with Ryan and Jacob) had to endure the hike to Illilouette Creek and back. My bad. Chris and Natalie, your support has meant the world. Jacob, your example gave me the courage to write, and for that I shall always be grateful.

34173043R00169

Made in the USA
Middletown, DE
13 August 2016